DEALINGS IN THE DARK

CURSED SOULS BOOK ONE

SAMANTHA MORAN

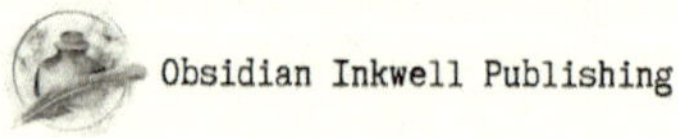

Titles: Dealings in the Dark / Samantha Moran
Description: Paperback Second Edition
Publication Date: October 26th, 2022
Cover Design: Samantha Moran (Canva)
Formatting: Samantha Moran (Vellum)

Paperback ISBN-13: 978-1-959751-00-7
Also available in ebook, hardcover, and audiobook editions.

DEDICATION

This novella is dedicated to my mother, Denise. You have always loved creepy stories. You are the reason I learned to enjoy the paranormal and not to fear the monsters on the page and screen. I love you, and I hope you enjoy this horror story written especially for you.

AUTHOR'S NOTE

Dealings in the Dark is an occult horror novella that deals with the dangerous consequences of magick. As such, the story you are about to read contains graphic scenes depicting physical violence, gore, mention of the death of a parent and grandparent, mention of child death and harm, limited depictions of dementia, and depictions of demonic creatures and forces. If any of these topics are disturbing to you, you may not wish to proceed with this text.

CURSED SOULS SERIES

Dealings in the Dark, 2022
Bound and Betrayed, 2022
Legacy of Lies, Coming Soon

PRAISE FOR DEALINGS IN THE DARK

The BookFest, Fall 2023
First Place Award Winner:
Supernatural Creatures and Beings

Author Shout Reader Ready Awards
Top Pick, 2024

"I loved this so much! I kept wanting to know what was going to happen next and it kept me at the edge of my seat. Wonderful horror novella!"
-R. Wyer

"This novella kept me up at night wanting to finish it all at once. Easy to read, and easy to "oooh" and "ahhh" at. If you like witchy anything, this is a great, quick read!"

-Marisol C.

"This was a riveting, fast-paced story. Ms. Moran's ability to paint a dark, hellish picture has few equals, if any. When all is said and done, you will absolutely need to pick up book two, Bound and Betrayed."

-Brian S.

"If you like all things spooky, supernatural, and witchy, this is the book to read! [...] I cannot wait for book #2! I need to know more about that ending!"

-Sarah B.

"When I heard the premise for *Dealings in the Dark* and saw the cover, I ran to find my Kindle! This was the perfect spooky season read to get me out of my slump [...] With the way this book ended, I cannot wait to read book two! The twist at the end of this was just phenomenal."

-Kassie G.

"...This novella had so many great moments that put you on the edge of your seat. This is a must read!"

-Marissa C.

"This novella is a fun, spooky read, perfect for a quiet and chilly autumn evening. It's got all sorts of goodies for lovers of the supernatural: a delightfully naughty demon of the crossroads, a practicing witch who happens to be desperate, a binding contract, running

water, bad decisions, an unexpected conclusion (which I did NOT see coming and thoroughly enjoyed), and a VERY bad dog. [...] Give this one a read."
	-Paul M.

TABLE OF CONTENTS

BONUS CONTENT: BOUND AND BETRAYED

CHAPTER ONE

THE BOX IN MY HAND RATTLES AS I QUICKLY WALK DOWN MY OLD ROAD beneath the light of an early autumn moon. The stars in the sky tonight are absolutely stunning. The air is still warm and humid, and the leaves have just begun to change. There is a refreshing breeze that causes the branches of the old willows to sway back and forth, almost as if they are dancing. The bits of gravel under my feet crunch against the soles of my worn Chucks, announcing my presence to anyone and anything that cares enough to listen.

Were I out here for any other reason, I might find my stroll enjoyable, leisurely even. I might listen to the frogs and crickets in the swampy underbrush tell their stories of the day. I might sit underneath one of the willows and drink a hot cider. I've done those things many times before.

But tonight, nothing about this walk is enjoyable. Every movement in the shadows makes me jump. Every crunch in the woods steals my breath and makes my whole body buzz with anxiety. I need to get this done, fast. The night is not safe anymore.

I hear a strangled whisper in the distance as the creature calls out my name. I'm not stupid enough to turn around and look, not this time. It almost had me before. I won't acknowledge it again. If I do, it will mean the end for me. The creature has caught my scent and has been stalking me for weeks. If it knows I can hear it, that I can see it, it will only make the hunt that much more thrilling. There will be no help for me.

I'm not ready to die.

The sounds of running water fill my ears as I approach the creek and the road veers sharply off to the left. I follow the path, staying as close to the water and as far away from the trees on the other side as the road allows.

For whatever reason, the creature is afraid of the water. Whenever I approach the creek, it always backs away. The sounds of its strangled cries grow softer as the creek burbles. I allow myself one deep breath to calm my nerves as I hug the water's edge. I relish the sense of momentary safety. It won't last long.

Before me, the road splits into a fork. To the left, it hugs the bank of the creek and promises continued safety, but that is not the path that I need to follow.

I hold the cigar box tightly to my chest as I test the wood of an old rickety bridge that leads off the right. I haven't crossed this bridge in years, not since I was young. The boards squeak in protest as I step forward, but to my relief, they bear my weight.

I move slowly, tip-toeing from one board to the next and stepping over the places where planks have fallen into the water below. The bridge isn't long or terribly high, and the creek isn't deep, but it is fast-moving right now, and if I were to fall in here, I would be in serious trouble. There's no one who would find me here, at least until the morning.

I'm running out of time. I don't know how long the water

will keep the beast at bay. Not indefinitely, I'm sure. I can't do this with the creature on my heels.

As I reach the end of the bridge and step onto the clay path on the other side, I desperately want to turn around to see if the beast has abandoned its hunt. My whole body fights to do so as I continue to force it forward toward my destination against every instinct of self-preservation. Out here, alone in the dark, I am easy prey, and leaving my back unguarded feels so very wrong.

I pick up speed, ducking underneath wild overgrowth and dodging debris from the last thunderstorm. The scents of decayed leaves and wet soil overwhelm my senses. I'm almost there. Almost.

Ahead, I can see my destination. Like a guardian, the old one-room schoolhouse looms over a four-way split in the path, the structure long since abandoned. In the light of the moon, it casts a shadow so long that the path is almost consumed. The school's double doors swing on their rusty hinges, grinding and groaning with the light breeze.

No one has cared for or claimed this space in years. It's perfect for what I must do now. There will be no interruptions or distractions.

Eager to reach my destination, I break into a run, and the rattling of the box intensifies as its contents bounce against the thin cedar sides. Thirty feet, twenty feet, ten. I skid to a halt at the center of the crossroads and fall to my knees, out of breath. Stones planted deep within the clay dig into my shins painfully, but I don't care. I made it to the crossing. The first part of my task is complete. I tentatively let out a sigh of relief.

I shift on my knees, twisting to retrieve an old spade and a lighter from my back pocket. I drop the lighter on the ground beside me. I use my hands to clear away the rocks and sticks in front of me before retrieving the spade and piercing it into the clay repeatedly, loosening the soil until I can dig up the earth and pile it by the side of the hole.

Once the hole is deep enough, I drop the spade beside the lighter and open the cigar box. I scan the contents again, just to make sure that nothing was lost on my journey. It's all there: dandelion leaves, wormwood, mandrake root, smoky quartz, a lock of my hair, a large black candle, and a small vial of my blood. I pull the candle out of the box and close it up, then place the box into the hole, burying it and patting the clay down firmly on top.

My hands shake as I place the candle atop the freshly turned earth. I close my eyes and feel for the lighter, lifting it up and squeezing it firmly in my hand. I pray to whoever might be listening that this will work. It has to. I don't know what else to do.

"I summon thee," I whisper my command. "Cross over into this plane. Hear me." I follow this with the difficult Latin words from my grandmother's near ancient grimoire, repeating them five times, then once more uttering my command. "I summon thee. Cross over into this plane."

I flick open the lid of the Zippo, springing to life a bright blue flame. Hesitantly, I tip the flame against the wick of the candle until it catches. Smoke curls up from the flame, gray and thick. It sparks, and the flame shoots high up into the air. Black wax drips down the side and puddles onto the clay below, spreading out from the candle and spilling toward me like a winding snake. I pull myself up from my knees to stand and watch as the wax drips farther and farther away from the source until it connects with my shoe. The ritual is working.

I take a step back, then skirt the candle and approach the old building. Cautiously, I scan the inside before entering. Old wood and metal tablet desks are tipped onto their sides. The place smells of mildew and rot. A large slate board, still bearing the marks of my childhood drawings, lines the farthest wall. Moonlight streams in through holes in the ceiling and the breeze whistles through spaces between the boards.

It's empty.

I close the doors firmly behind me as I step inside, shoving an old, busted table in front of them to keep them from opening of their own accord. It isn't much, but I hope that it will at least slow the creature down when it finds me. I just need it to buy me time.

It's quiet in the one-room schoolhouse. Only the sounds of my breathing and the creaking beneath my shoes echo in the large, abandoned space. I squeeze my black tourmaline and obsidian necklace for protection, a gift from my grandmother, as I pick my way through the remains of the once-loved class-room until I reach the slate board, as far away from the doors as I can be, and I wait. I close my eyes, breathing as quietly as I can, and listen.

Moments later, a deep chuckle behind me tells me I am not alone.

CHAPTER TWO

"Well, hello there," a discordant voice sounds from behind me. "What are you doing all the way out here, and in the middle of the night, I might add? You're a *long* way from home."

My breath catches in my chest and my blood runs cold. I feel my resolve seep out of me as a heavy dread rises up to take its place. Even though I performed the ritual for this exact purpose, every instinct I possess tells me to get out of here, to run as fast as I can and never look back. Yet, as my nature begs me to flee, I find myself turning slowly to face him. The floor creaks ominously beneath my shifting weight.

In the shadowy corner, his tall, thin figure leans casually against the chipped and flaking wood paneling. Despite his apathetic stance, something in his posture feels predatory, like a cat watching its prey, waiting for it to make a move so the hunt can begin. My gaze shoots from his polished black boots up to his steepled fingers, held just beneath his pointed chin. The shadows obscure most of his features, but his burning eyes penetrate the darkness, glowing faintly red.

"What? No welcome? I came a very long way to see you tonight, Alex." The figure pushes himself up and away from the wall gracefully. He tilts his head to the side, watching me closely. When I don't move, rooted in place by my fear, a wide, malicious grin breaks across his face. Razorsharp teeth gleam white in the moonlight.

The sight causes me to take a step backward, and I feel the old slate board press into me as I flatten my back against the far wall. "Iroth," I whisper.

"In the flesh!" he squeals happily, dancing forward. He claps his hands together, then with a flourish, turns in place as though showing off his new attire. "Well, someone's flesh, anyway. I borrowed the visage. How do you like it? It was chosen especially for you."

"I don't."

At this, his face twists into an image of childlike disappointment, lips pouting and brows furrowed. "But, I thought you liked this face, Pet. You did when we were young. I sought him out. I found him again! Sure, it's a bit older now, but..."

"I am not young anymore, and I know what you are," I interrupt forcefully. I lock eyes with him, drawing up every shred of courage I possess.

"Of course," he nods condescendingly. He reaches down and rights an overturned desk, then slides easily into the seat, throwing his legs up on the wooden table. "How could I have forgotten? You must forgive me. It's been *so* long."

"Not long enough."

He huffs indignantly. "If you don't want to play with me, Alex, why did you summon me here? I thought we were going to have some fun. Now, it seems like I may need to make my own. You know how I abhor boredom." Iroth leans forward slightly in challenge. "Don't you want to play? We could paint this forest with blood if you'd like. All you have to do is ask, and I'll show you how to have a good time."

"We have very different ideas of what constitutes fun, Iroth. I won't make that mistake again. You preyed on an innocent little girl. You took advantage of my ignorance. I'm not so naive now."

"Innocent?" he asks in mock astonishment. "Hardly. Anyway, as I recall, you were the one who told me that the girl deserved whatever was coming to her. You hated her. I only handled the problem."

"I was nine years old!" I retort. "I didn't know who you were or what you were going to do. It was a childhood feud, and you ripped her to shreds right in front of me!"

He leans back once more and picks at his pointed black nails. "Yes, well. I don't see her bothering you anymore. What was her name? Cassandra? Megan?"

"Selena." My voice catches as I whisper her name, a name I have tried to forget for many, many years.

"Yes! Selena!" he answers, feigning sudden realization with a snap of his fingers. "What a beautiful name. She and I had such fun together. I'll remember the experience fondly for all of my days." When I make no move to respond, he adjusts the lapels on his crisp black blazer and stares back at me. "Come, sit with me. Apparently, we have matters to discuss."

Iroth motions his hand lazily at another desk, and a thick red stream of smoke shoots out from underneath the cuff of his sleeve, lifting the desk and slamming it down in front of him with an echoing thud. It spins to face him, scarring the old wooden floor.

A second stream of smoke shoots out from his other sleeve and snatches me around the waist, drawing me closer to him with impossible force. I resist, digging the heels of my worn shoes into the wood and scrambling for purchase as I slide helplessly past the abandoned schoolmaster's desk, but it's futile. The tendril lifts me into the air and dumps me unceremoniously into the desk chair. The impact is jarring, and already I can feel a bruise forming on my tailbone. I growl at him in frustration, and this only makes him laugh.

"Tell me, Alex. Why am I here? I do have things to attend to, you know? Deals to make, souls to collect, people to kill. What could you possibly want?"

The old desk is small, and I struggle to arrange myself, spinning to tuck my legs beneath the table. I grip the seat's edges firmly, trying to push myself out of it, but I find myself incapable of standing. Whatever magic he used to deposit me here remains, wrapped around my arms and legs, pinning them down. I am as helpless to escape his grip now as I had been all those years ago. Frustrated, I blow a piece of my hair out of my eyes and snap, "I want you to call off your beast."

"Which beast?" he asks innocently. He lifts his eyebrows and tilts his head to the side. "I have so many. You will have to be much, much more specific, Pet."

Annoyance begins to override my fear, and though I know that I should tread carefully with him, I spit, "The one that's eating all of my chickens and stalking me through the woods at night. The one that reeks of rotten eggs and burns footprints into my front porch. You know, the one that chased me nearly a mile three days ago and tried to break into my house. That one!"

"Oh, oh, oh," he taunts, laughing maliciously. "You must mean CeCe. She is a feisty little thing. In fact, she's one of my favorites."

"CeCe?" I scoff.

"What? You don't like the name? I find it quite amusing."

I struggle to break free of the desk once more, unwilling to be the subject of his derision. "I... don't care... what the stupid hound's... name is!" I grunt. "Ugh!" I should have known better than to fight my restraints, but my stubbornness and anger are getting the best of me. Out of breath, I demand, "Just call it off and leave me the hell alone."

"That wasn't the deal," he says, suddenly serious. He reaches into the pocket of his blazer and retrieves a roll of parchment. On either end, ornate copper metalwork, patinated with age, sparks. The parchment releases, rolling down to the floor and away from Iroth, slowing to a stop as it bumps against my toes. "See?"

"What deal?" I ask, incredulous. "I never made a deal with you."

"Oh, but you did," he says, voice laced with venom. "And now, Pet, I'm calling it in. You can read it if you'd like. It's all there, signed in your very own blood. Mmm," he inhales. "It still smells so delicious."

Iroth waves his hand, and the invisible force restraining me lightens. I lean forward and scoop up the end of the roll of parchment, squinting and straining to read the heavily slanted cursive. There at the bottom, written in dried crimson, is my name: Alexandria Clare Hendricks.

"I never signed this!" I shout, irate. "What is this, Iroth?"

"Our arrangement!" he laughs, amusement returning to his features. He gestures toward the parchment and it abruptly rolls itself back around the thin copper bar. He gingerly tucks the contract back into his pocket with a smirk. As if quoting the text, using a voice that perfectly mimics my own nine-year-old self, he says, "I, Alexandria Clare Hendricks, agree to abide by the terms and agreements of this contract, to be completed at such a time and in such a manner as required by Iroth, demon of the abyss. I bind the contract with my blood and stake upon it my mortal soul should the terms and agreements not be satisfied in full."

"I would have remembered signing a contract with you!" I yell. Furious, I try to stand and step forward, but the invisible force of Iroth's magic returns, slamming me backward in my seat so violently that the desk skitters several feet across the floor. The force of the impact steals my breath. I sputter and cough, trying to reclaim the lost air.

"You would think so, yes," he states, watching me. "After all, I remember it so clearly. Poor little Selena, lying dead in a thick, sticky puddle of her own blood in the middle of your grandmother's basement. I did some of my best work on her, you know. Dismemberment is tricky sometimes. So, when you demanded that I fix it and bring her back... well, I was absolutely disheartened. I wanted you to like it, Pet. I did it all for you."

I open my mouth to speak, but one sharp look from him has me closing it again.

"You begged me to bring her back to life. Don't you remember?"

"Of course. I..."

"And I did that, didn't I?"

"Yes, but..."

"And before that, do you remember when I sat down beside you and offered you my blade?"

I struggle to reach back through eighteen years of repressed memories, memories I have spent years in therapy trying to forget. Then, Iroth snaps his fingers. The scene from my childhood appears before us, like a misty movie projected into the thin air. Iroth leans back, watching with glee.

THERE IS SO MUCH BLOOD. The carpet is soaked. It makes squelching sounds as I run forward to Selena, horrified. I feel it squish between my toes and coat the soles of my feet. I sob and sob, all while Iroth, whom I believed to be a young boy of my age named Carter, watches with an evil smirk. I beg and plead for Selena to wake up. I barely understand what I am seeing. Things that should have been inside of her are splayed out around her like morbid wings. I try to stuff it back in. The smell... oh, the smell. Then... there's the knife. He offers it to me, and I stare at him, seeing for the first time what he really is.

"Do you really want her to come back?" Iroth, then Carter, asks. "I can bring her back for you. All you have to do is owe me a favor. That's not so bad, right?"

"A favor?" I sniffle, trying to wipe away tears and smearing blood across my cheeks.

"Just a favor. Nothing more," he answers, reaching into his backpack and pulling out a small, spiral-bound notebook. "If you prick your finger and put it right here, I can bring her back, and all you'll owe me is one little favor, okay? Do you want to do that?"

"You'll bring her back?"

"I'll bring her back, though if you ask me, it seems like such a waste. It's your decision. A favor for Selena's life, or..." he points, "she stays like this."

I nod and extend my hand, accepting Iroth's blade.

As I prick my finger, Iroth hungrily snatches it up, squeezing a droplet of blood onto the college-ruled paper and pressing my finger down, leaving a bloody print behind. Before my eyes, I see the fingerprint shift and change. The swirls expand and contract until they form the wet, crimson letters of my own name.

Iroth waves his hand over the padlet and it morphs into the

roll of parchment, which he quickly stuffs inside of his backpack.

With a wave of his hand, the gruesome carnage before my younger self disappears. Selena stirs behind us, clutching her stomach and chest, eyes wide with terror. She looks up at me, and when her eyes fall on Iroth, she screams, sliding herself back into the corner with her feet and covering her head.

I run to her to comfort her, but she cowers and shrinks away from my touch. She rocks back and forth, back and forth, back and forth. I look back to where Carter had been, but he is gone, nowhere to be seen as if he had never even been there in the first place. I scramble over to the house phone and call 9-1-1.

The paramedics come first, then the police. My friend is loaded onto a stretcher and strapped down.

After they take her away, I never see Selena again.

I MADE A DEAL WITH IROTH. How had I forgotten?

"As you can see, Pet, you did indeed make a bargain with me," Iroth asserts, his voice breaking through my haze. He waves his hand once more and the misty image dissolves.

"I was nine! I didn't know what I was doing. You murdered my friend, and I just wanted her back. You preyed on me. You used me."

"Be that as it may," he replies, swiftly rising and approaching me with that same catlike grace, "you made a deal. You signed it in blood. You placed your own mortal soul as collateral. And now, after all these years, it's time for you to pay up. I'm calling in your contract, Alex. So, what will it be? Are you going to do that teensy little favor for me, the one that you promised to do all those years ago, or are you going to hand over your soul? I'm sure CeCe would be thrilled to collect it for me."

At this, the doors to the schoolhouse burst open, splintered wood spraying into the room. I duck, barely dodging a huge chunk of debris. It slams into the old slate board behind me and fractures into little pieces. With a heavy thud, the remaining wood falls to the floor, ripped off of its hinges.

Burning eyes appear first, then hulking, churning shadows emerge, blowing out steaming breath. The shadows quickly coalesce into the solid form of a muscle-bound, spiny hound. Patches of flesh have been ripped away from the beast's side, exposing shining bone and fibrous tissue beneath the creature's skin.

The scents of rotting flesh and sulfur fill the room, making my head spin and threatening to force me to revisit my last meal. I cover my nose and scoot the desk away, but Iroth approaches me menacingly. He leans forward until his face is almost touching my own, pinning me to the desk with his hands on either side of the chair.

"You choose, Pet," he says with a sick smile. "Either hold up your end of the deal or be ripped to shreds by my favorite hound. I'll have fun either way."

CHAPTER THREE

I watch helplessly as the hound stalks forward, head low to the ground with its mangled and pointed ears tipped back, teeth gnashing and grinding.

Iroth releases his grip on the chair and moves to stand behind me, leaving the space between myself and the beast wide open. I'm exposed and vulnerable, and panic sets in as the beast snaps its gaping mouth and licks its lips.

Firmly grabbing my shoulders, Iroth shoves me even farther back into the seat. He stares down at me, face split from ear to ear in a manic grin. His pointed black nails dig into my flesh, puncturing my clothes and sinking deep into my muscle. I struggle to free myself from his grasp, but between the invisible bonds and his powerful hands, my efforts are futile. Iroth laughs mercilessly as I wriggle like a worm on a hook.

The hound's huge claws leave long, deep gouges in the rotting wood with each heavy step. Thick, blood-tinged slime and foaming drool leaks out of its mouth, forming a disgusting trail along the floor. I grunt and desperately pull at Iroth's hands, but he digs his nails in deeper each time I resist.

"I'm so very glad that you called me here tonight, Pet. I had intended to leave the theatrics to CeCe alone, but what a show I would have missed. The sound of your terror is absolute music to my ears," Iroth sings, leaning in closer until his face is only inches from my own. "There's nothing like feeling you squirm beneath my grasp. You know, I have an entire legion of agonized souls in my domain, but you... well, you are my favorite. I cannot wait to add you to the collection. We will spend eternity enjoying little games like these. Doesn't that sound grand?"

"I..." I force myself to grind out, "do... not belong... to you!"

I heave my body forward and somehow break away from Iroth's grip, overturning the desk and rolling away, landing on my side with a resounding thump. Even away from his grasp, the unseen restraints remain.

Above me, Iroth rubs his hands together as if cleaning off grime. "Not yet," he says confidently. "But, you will."

He returns to his desk and sits down, watching me with unabashed interest. His expression is saturated with amusement as he leans off to the side and almost lovingly swipes his hand along the hound's boney spine.

"You are a stubborn one," he muses. "I thought I was about to experience an entire evening of absolute boredom, and yet, I find that I will thoroughly enjoy watching her snap your bones and devour your flesh. That is unless you would like to follow through with our little arrangement. It's your choice, of course. What will it be?"

The hound reaches me, bringing its head down level with my own. It roars, and my skin crawls as its putrid, moist breath blows across my face, reeking of death. I gag and try to turn my body away, continuing to struggle against my bonds.

The beast stands on its haunches, and hot drool slips down onto my face. I see its swift movement, but I do not have enough time or mobility to react. It raises its front paw high into the air, then slams it down on my leg with the full weight of its body.

I scream as searing pain blasts through me, spasming as the bone snaps and my flesh rips open. Blood spurts, then oozes out onto the floor. Horrified, I see the creature lower its head and lap my blood up off the floor.

Iroth leans back in his chair, grinning wickedly at the intensity of my pain. "Are you ready to discuss my terms?"

"Arragh!" I yell, trying and failing to tear my leg away from the hound. It simply places its paw on top of my thigh, rendering my leg incapable of movement, then sinks its fangs deep into my flesh. I scream again, and the creature growls, then tugs me closer, dragging me across the floor with its powerful jaws.

"What I require of you is really quite simple," Iroth continues. He raises his eyebrows and tilts his face as the hound shakes its head violently, teeth still sunk deep into my muscles, shredding them. "Consider it a scavenger hunt, if you will. Someone has something that I want, and all you have to do is claim it for me."

"What do you want?" I cry through excruciating pain as the hound clamps down even harder. Its razorsharp fangs scrape against my bone, sending brutal vibrations zinging through my body.

"Mmm, so she can be reasonable," he quips. "I didn't know if you had it in you."

The hound growls deeply once more, but Iroth shushes it.

"Down girl," he commands. "All in good time."

It releases my leg and turns to face him, blowing hot steam impatiently into the air, then whips its head back to me, pressing its short, scaly nose into my own.

"Ah! CeCe, you bad, bad girl. I said DOWN!"

The building shakes with the volume of his command. Dust drifts lazily down from the ceiling, sparkling with ironic beauty in the moonlight as the vicious creature reluctantly backs away and curls up at Iroth's feet. Its eyes flare red and orange as it regards me with obvious hunger.

I force my own eyes away and watch as my blood soaks the floor, dripping between the cracks of the boards. Though I try to contain it, I can't help but whimper at the burning ache in my thigh. I will my leg to move, but as hard as I try, it remains static.

Traitorous tears slide down my face as I cast my eyes back to Iroth. He's leaning forward with his elbows on his knees, looking for all the world as though this is the happiest night of his life.

"What do you want?" I whimper. "What do you want?"

"Something that was taken from me long, long ago, Pet. A ring. Just a little, silver ring. It's mine, and I will have it back. You will retrieve it for me."

"A ring?" I groan. "You would kill me for a stupid ring?"

Anger flashes across his features so quickly that I almost miss it. "It is *not* a stupid ring."

In response to his anger, the hound rises from the floor and towers over me threateningly. I flinch, but Iroth guides it back down beside him. He strokes its head absently, and the creature nuzzles into him with a snort.

"What's so important," I grit out as agony once more flashes through me, "about this ring? Why would you try to kill me for it?"

"That," he says, relaxing back into his casual state and tapping his fingers on the table, "is not important. And Pet, I think you forget that I would absolutely love to kill you regardless. I've learned a few new tricks since I visited you last, and I'm just *dying* to show you. Should I allow CeCe to demonstrate one of my newest hobbies? See, it involves something like making balloon animals, but with your — "

"That will *NOT* be necessary," I hiss angrily, clutching at my thigh to slow the bleeding. "How am I supposed to find your ring, anyway?"

"I'm certain that finding it will be easy enough," he says without even a hint of concern. "After all, it is currently in your grandmother's possession. How's that for a simple task, Pet? All you need to do is take it from her and return it to me."

A mirthless laugh escapes my lips before I can call it back. "If you know where it is, why don't you just go get it yourself?"

"Alas, I cannot," he answers, irritation clear in his expression. "After our last encounter, your grandmother warded herself and your home against me. And my ring. In fact, she warded you against me as well. That has proven a particular puzzle for me, as I intended to satisfy our contract ages ago, but try as I might, you were just out of my reach. It seems that your summoning spell tonight finally allowed me access to you. I should have sent CeCe after you years ago. If I had known you would cave to the pressure so quickly..."

I wince as the full force of my own stupidity sets in. I thought summoning Iroth was my only escape from the hell-hound, but it was a trap, one I too easily stepped into. I should have known better. How could I have been so foolish?

"Anyway," he says with a sigh, "as much as it will pain me, if you bring me what I desire, I will spare your life. Bring me my ring, and I will destroy your contract. You'll be free to live the rest of your miserable, human life without wondering if I will ever darken your door again."

The slick, hot blood continues to seep out of my wounds, sliding through my fingers. I focus on my breathing, trying to slow my racing heart in hopes of staunching the flow. I'm beginning to feel cold and clammy. A shiver sets in and my teeth clack together loudly. I allow my eyes to roll back into my head for just a moment, then force them to open. The darkness of sleep is calling to me, but I know that if I give in now, that will be it. I won't let that happen.

"I can't find your damn ring if you let me bleed out on the floor," I spit with as much venom as I possess. "Iroth, help me."

"So, you'll follow through with your part of the bargain then?" he asks. His eyes narrow and snag my own. He slides out of the desk and onto the floor, then crouches over me possessively. "You've made your choice?"

"I'll find your ring."

"Oh, goody!" he shouts. I flinch again as he claps and flourishes his hand, waving it over my body. Surges of lightning spark through my skin, and I shriek, unable to control myself. My bones snap back into place like puzzle pieces. My muscles reform and my skin stitches itself back together. I seize up in the face of such intense pain, and when I feel the invisible bonds slacken, I immediately roll to my side and vomit, expelling every ounce of my stomach without shame.

"There. All better, Pet. That's all you had to say. A deal's a deal, after all."

I snap my head back to Iroth and glower, pure fury flowing out of my eyes so intensely that I'm sure he can feel it. He drags his finger through the puddle of my blood on the floor, then brings it to his lips and licks the crimson liquid off, smacking his lips in delight.

"You are delicious in every way. I almost hope you fail, Alex. I would love to devour you *completely*."

I shudder as he rises and backs away, retreating toward the door.

"Two days," he says without looking back. "I expect my ring will be returned before the height of the full moon. If it's not..." he says, stopping.

He snaps his fingers, and the hound, who has been waiting patiently by his seat, surges toward me and shoves me back against the floor, bearing down on my chest with its meaty paws and pricking my skin with its claws.

The paws begin to burn, searing my flesh as they have the wood of my porch. I scream again as my skin sizzles beneath them. The smell of burnt flesh fills my nose as the hound backs away, leaving me spellbound on the floor.

"I'm sure I do not have to remind you of the fate that awaits you should you fail," he continues. "CeCe will keep watch over you to ensure that you are indeed following through on our deal. You'll meet me here in two nights' time with the ring in hand, or I will claim your soul, Pet. I'll be... around."

I struggle to my feet, clutching the burns on my chest tightly. "What if I need your help?" I ask, unsure what else to say.

"Don't," is all he says before waving his hand at CeCe, who bounds toward him. He turns to face me and bows flamboyantly before stepping out into the night, leaving me speechless and alone in the middle of the schoolhouse.

CHAPTER FOUR

The walk home from the crossroads feels so much longer than my hurried journey only hours before. Though most of the injuries I sustained in the dilapidated schoolhouse have been healed, my muscles ache with strain and exhaustion.

The patches of scorched skin from the hellhound's enormous paws sting and throb with every feather-light touch of the remnants of my shirt. Unphased by the considerably cooler early morning air, by the time I am nearly halfway home, I opt to discard the shirt altogether rather than endure the pain unnecessarily. Gingerly, I withdraw my arms from the tattered fabric and wad it into a ball, tossing it unceremoniously into the creek. I watch numbly as the current, sped along by the week's earlier rain, snatches it up and carries it away into the night.

My Chucks leave long scuffs in the dirt as I drag my feet, nearly collapsing onto the road several times. The shock and adrenaline of our encounter have worn thin, and the sweet smell of the lilac bushes just across the bridge and the gurgling current of the water threaten to drag me into a deep, dreamless sleep.

Finally, reaching my porch, I heave myself up each step with considerable effort until I can grab a hold of my door. My numb fingers fumble with my keys, but I manage to twist them in the lock and let myself inside. The large wall clock reads 2:07 am as I shut the door behind me and secure it once more.

Barely able to keep my eyes open, I drop my keys onto the entry table and trail my hands along the wall until I stand before the set of stairs that leads up to my room. In my weary state, the stairs seem to stretch longer and longer before me, creating a nauseating optical illusion.

There is absolutely no way I can climb the stairs tonight. Instead, I turn toward the living room and lug myself over to the couch where I promptly collapse, falling face first onto the soft fabric, muddy shoes and bloody clothes forgotten. Within seconds, I am lost to slumber.

A sharp knock at my door startles me out of a sleep so deep that I barely recognize my surroundings when I wake. For a moment, the room spins so quickly that bile begins to creep up my throat. After several deep, steadying breaths, I slowly use my arms to push myself up until I am seated and rub my eyes to clear away the waking haze.

It's later than I thought it would be. Sun streams brightly through the bay window overlooking my front lawn. I squint my eyes at it in frustration. In my haste, I had forgotten to close the curtains before venturing off to the crossroads, and I am paying for that oversight now. Though I had absolutely nothing to drink last night, I feel incredibly hungover. My brain throbs with a migraine more intense than any I have ever experienced before.

I groan as the nuisance at the front door knocks again, louder this time. As I move to rise, a flash of heat across the tight skin of my chest reminds me of the pain I endured last night at Iroth's bidding. I look down at the burn, only to see that I never put on another shirt.

"Great," I mutter.

I search the room for anything I can use to cover myself, finding only my grandmother's favorite throw. I cringe at the realization that I am absolutely filthy, covered in dirt and gore. As I haul it up over my shoulders and wrap it tightly around myself, I silently promise her that I will wash the throw later, feeling guilty for yet another stupid choice. It seems that I am incapable of doing the right thing lately.

I stand and steady myself, holding firm to the arm of the couch to find my balance, then make my way back through the entryway and up to the front door. The unwelcome visitor knocks again as I slide the heavy metal cover away from the peephole and peer outside. It's the postal worker, looking quite annoyed, and holding a small box under his arm. I roll my eyes and open the door just a crack, shielding them from the sun.

"Sorry, Jameson. I'm not moving very quickly today."

The young postal worker, no older than thirty-five, traces his eyes from my face down to my feet and back before raising his eyebrows and smiling. All hints of annoyance disappear from his face, replaced by a knowing look.

"Late night?" he asks with a chuckle, clearly amused.

"You have no idea."

"Yeah, been there," he answers. "Partying gets harder after twenty-five. At least, for me it did."

He waits for me to laugh, but I don't. Even though Jameson is nice enough and means no harm, I have no interest in this conversation today. All I want is for him to leave so I can shut this door and drain an entire pot of coffee, followed closely by a bottle of ibuprofen.

"Well, I've got a package for you," he says, giving up on

small talk. "It says that you need to sign for it. Sorry to wake you up."

I nod and say nothing. Jameson pulls a scanner out of his pocket and holds it out to me, pulling a little black stylus away from the side. I fumble with the stylus and sloppily sign my name, then pass it back to him, hands shaking.

"Alright, all set," he says, stuffing the scanner back into his pocket and holding out the package.

I ease the door open farther, just enough so that the box slides through the crack, careful not to drop the throw in the process. If I survive this deal with Iroth, the last thing I need is to be ogled by the mailman every time he stops by.

"Get some sleep, okay? You look like you could use it."

I nod, leaning my head against the door frame and staring down at his shoes.

Taking the hint, Jameson tips his hat to me and walks away, whistling as he goes. I watch as he climbs back into his little white van and disappears, leaving a trail of dust as he reaches the end of the drive, and turns out onto the main road.

As soon as I shut the door behind me, my stomach churns and bubbles, the pressure rising up, up, up. I quickly drop the throw and the package, racing upstairs to the bathroom and barely making it to the toilet before I heave up what little contents are left in my stomach. Cold sweat breaks out across my body as I lower myself onto the tile floor and try to calm my racing heart. It beats so vigorously that a cramp forms beneath my sternum. I breathe through the pain until the stitch lets go, reigning in the lingering panic from the night before.

I rinse my mouth and brush my teeth in an attempt to clear the sour taste before starting a cold shower. I abandon my soiled clothing on the floor and step inside, wincing at each drop of pounding water that slips across the burns and watching as the dirt runs in rivulets down the drain. I scrub, and scrub, and scrub until the rest of my body feels as raw as the wound on my chest, but no matter how much I try to erase the events of the night before, I can still feel Iroth's pointed nails digging into my shoulders and the bite of the hound's enormous jaws ripping into my flesh. A shiver that has nothing to do with the temperature of the water wracks my body and goosebumps erupt across my skin.

"Stupid. That was so incredibly stupid!" I yell in frustration at no one but myself. "I should have brought more protection than my necklace. I know better than to panic and rush into things, especially with a demon. Stupid. Stupid. Stupid!"

Ashamed, I twist the knobs to halt the water's flow and reach for my towel, wrapping it tightly around myself and exiting the shower. Still dripping, I scoop up the dirty clothes from the floor and reluctantly toss them into the trash, my favorite Chucks included. The clothes are torn and stained, and I don't need the reminder of what awaits me if I should fail to find Iroth's ring before the full moon.

I towel off quickly and run my fingers through my hair, leaving trails in their wake. Then, I dab salve across the burn and cover it with gauze before padding down the hall to my room to get dressed. I choose the softest, most comfortable material I can find, a well-worn black cotton shirt and old jeans. Over this, I layer a plaid button-down shirt. I cuff my jeans at the ankles, then stuff my feet into a thin pair of socks and a holey pair of black canvas flats before stepping back into the hall and descending the stairs to retrieve my grandmoth-er's throw and the package.

Absently, I carry the throw to the laundry room and toss it into the large pile of dirty laundry waiting to be washed, then head back to the couch and sit down to examine the box.

There's no return address, only my name written in ethe-real red loops across the top. Seeing this, I frown. I haven't ordered anything recently, and the handwriting is strange, old even. I peel the tape off of the top flaps and open it up, digging through crumpled newspaper to discover what is hidden inside.

To my surprise, it's another, smaller box. This one is sleek and black with hinges, matte to the touch. As I open the lid, a folded piece of paper falls into my lap, revealing a shining silver pocket watch. I lift the watch up by the chain and dangle it in front of me, inspecting it. Light glints off of the polished exterior as it spins. On the front, engraved between elaborate swirls, is my name: Alexandria. The slanting script is beautiful, yet I find the watch unnerving as it quietly ticks, interrupting the silence of the space.

"What the hell?" I ask, turning it over in my hands. "Who sent me a pocket watch?"

Gently, I place the watch back into the small black box and shut the lid, setting it down beside me. I unfold the small piece of paper to find a note in the same ethereal writing as the address on the outer package. It reads:

Alexandria,

I had such fun playing with you last night. What a wonderful evening we shared! Alas, I cannot be with you today, as I have further business to attend to. Rest assured, CeCe is nearby to keep an eye on you in my absence. She's simply salivating at the thought of spending the next couple of days with you!

I thought you might need a little reminder that you are now rapidly approaching a very important deadline, Tick tock, Pet. Your time is running out. I cannot wait to play with you again. What fun CeCe and I shall have!

Find the ring and bring it to me, or we will rend the flesh from your bones while you watch. Either way, I'm looking forward to seeing you soon. Kisses!

Your best friend,

Iroth

DISGUSTED, I crumple the note and toss it into the larger package. As I do, I catch sight of something that steals the breath from my lungs.

My hands tremble as I withdraw one of the newspaper balls and spread it out across my lap. In huge, bold letters, the headline reads: **LOCAL GIRL FOUND IN HYSTERICS IN FRIEND'S BASEMENT, AUTHORITIES UNABLE TO MAKE SENSE OF IT**. I read on, knowing exactly what I will find.

Wednesday afternoon, emergency rescue received a call regarding a young girl whom a friend described as incredibly frightened. Upon arrival, Selena Thomas, aged 10, was found in hysterics, unresponsive to medical personnel. Paramedics removed her from the scene of the incident, a basement belonging to local Elizabeth Hendricks, aged 52, whose granddaughter, aged 9, reported the incident to 9-1-1.

Police arrived on the scene to investigate shortly after the paramedics, but as of now, they have found no indication of a break-in or foul play. Police Chief Smith released the following statement this morning:

"The child in question, Selena Thomas, has been admitted to the local hospital for psychiatric care. Though our EMTs did their best to calm her and find out what exactly occurred, all we know right now is that the child claims to have been the victim of a brutal physical attack. We have found no evidence to support this claim. If you know anything about an incident that may have occurred this Wednesday in or around the Hendricks home, we urge you to come forward."

Selena Thomas has been placed under twenty-four-hour watch in our local psychiatric unit to ensure her safety in the aftermath of these mysterious events. Police continue to try to coax more information from the victim, but have little hope that the victim, given her state of shock, will produce anything further. If you know anything that may be helpful to authorities, please call the local hotline at 637-555-9672.

UNNERVED, I throw the newspaper article aside and retrieve another crumpled ball, unfurling it to see that it is the exact same article as the last. The scraps fall to the floor as I inspect them all. Piece after piece of the same article has been crumpled and stuffed into the package, a torment designed just for me.

"You sick bastard," I say as I look down at the clippings, toeing them aside with my shoe. Hot tears threaten to break free as I stare at them, guilt consuming me. He has planned this perfectly, intent on torturing me even while he's not here. Unwilling to give him the satisfaction, I shake my head and pick the papers up off the floor, tossing them into the old gas fireplace and twisting the knob to ignite it.

As the papers catch fire, the horrifying sound of Selena's shrill, ear-splitting screams pierces the air, a perfect replica. I stumble backward, eyes wide with terror. My whole body trembles as the flames rise higher, licking the edges of the cobblestone enclosure and leaving scorch marks behind. Before me, the flames flash vibrant red and purple, then morph into a twisted image of Iroth's smirking face. His visage winks at me before dying down with a flash.

I grip the edge of the couch to hold myself upright, but the scraps of paper only smolder and smoke in the hearth. Iroth is nowhere to be seen. It doesn't take long for the clippings to be reduced to crumbling ash. All that remains of Iroth's magic is the thick scent of sulfur that permeates the room in its wake.

"Ugh, I hate you!" I shout, hoping that wherever he is, he can hear me. I glare at the fireplace, waiting for a response of some kind, but the room remains silent.

Satisfied that the flames will not suddenly leap back to life, I throw open the side panes of the bay window to release the horrendous smell.

What I expect to be fresh, late morning air is far more fetid than the stink of the room itself. I gag and slam the windows shut, noticing the deep, wide paw prints sunk into the wet ground just below. The beast is nowhere to be seen, but it has been here recently. I search the shadowy tree line for its hulking shape and come up empty. With a defeated sigh, I cross the room, mumbling obscenities about Iroth as I do so.

Just as I am about to pass the threshold into the hall, I hear a metallic zing and turn to see a flash of silver flying straight toward me. Before I can duck, the pocket watch strikes me hard on the arm and falls to my feet. I wince and rub at the spot where it hit me, bewildered.

On the floor below, the watch wobbles gently, as innocuous as a pocket watch can be. I stare at it for a moment, then, testing a theory, step one foot lightly into the hall. It trails behind me, skittering across the wood floor. I back away again, this time a little farther, and again it follows, like a dog on a leash. With a sigh, I bend down and pick it up. At my touch, the watch vibrates subtly and grows noticeably warmer.

"I take it I am not meant to leave you behind," I say, annoyed.

The gears of the watch grind loudly. I take this as confirmation. Of course, Iroth wants to continue his sick little game, reminding me constantly of his presence, as if I could possibly forget. I squeeze it tightly in my hand, contemplating throwing it through the window, but drop it into my pocket instead. The last thing I need now is an inanimate object trying to decapitate me.

With the watch tucked safely into my shirt pocket, I walk to the entry table in the hall and snatch up my keys, then leave the house, locking the door behind me. The clock is literally ticking, as Iroth wishes so keenly to remind me, and I have to find this damn ring before my time runs out.

I climb into my Jeep and turn the ignition, throwing it into drive. Just as I'm about to turn out onto the main road, a hard thump near my back tire shakes my car. A low growl sounds below my window, but when I peer outside, there is nothing there.

Awareness seeps in as I stare at the empty space outside my car door: the hound, my infernal babysitter, possesses the gift of invisibility. That's why I couldn't see it before. Now, it's making its presence known and flaunting my weakness. I cannot fight what I cannot see, and the beast knows this, too.

I swing my Jeep out onto the road and slam on the gas in an attempt to leave it behind, but in the rearview mirror, its hulking figure trails behind me, made visible only by the displacement it causes in the dust. This beast keeps pace perfectly. Any hope of escaping my infernal guardian fades away. Apparently, I won't be visiting my grandmother alone.

CHAPTER FIVE

The muffled sound of my grandmother shuffling her tarot cards greets me as I weave between nurses and visiting families in the solarium. Unsurprisingly, I find her in her favorite spot, nestled in the corner between a large window and several tall potted plants. Her best altar cloth is spread before her, a deep burgundy velvet square that covers the little wooden table, and her favorite aide is sitting across from her, staring intently at the spread as she places the cards down purposefully on the cloth.

I watch as she squints her eyes at each one in turn, tracing the familiar imagery with the tip of her finger. She taps the last card and says, "No, it isn't worth it. I think you knew that when you asked me, though. Walk away from that man, Zachariah. He's no good."

"When you're right, you're right," Zachariah agrees, nodding his head thoughtfully. "Thank you, Ms. Hendricks. I needed to hear that today."

Zachariah stands, straightening his scrubs. When he looks

in my direction, he flashes me a quick smile and waves me over to them.

I smile back and watch as my grandmother collects the spread with her long, knobby fingers. She reverently returns them to the rest of her deck and shuffles again, bridging them, spreading them, and bridging them once more, before placing the deck back down on the velvety cloth.

"Is she having a good day?" I whisper to Zachariah before my grandmother notices me.

"I'd say we're somewhere in the middle right now," he answers. His expression is full of pity when my grandmother looks up, finally seeing me standing there. "You've got a visitor, Ms. Hendricks. Your granddaughter Alex is here to see you."

At first, it seems like she doesn't quite recognize me. Then, a flash of recognition flares in her eyes. "Oh, I know who she is," my grandmother responds with a dismissive wave. "Come over here, Alex. Sit with me for a while."

Zachariah waves politely as he takes his leave, and I slide into the now vacant chair across from my grandmother. My eyes follow him as he strides across the solarium and sits with another resident who appears to be playing chess by themselves, joining them in their game.

"Where have you been, child?" my grandmother asks me. She leans back in her creaky chair and studies me, her expression unreadable.

"I've been a bit preoccupied as of late," I tell her, keeping my voice low so that no one else can hear us. "A certain someone sent a very unwelcome creature to keep watch over me for the last few weeks, and I didn't want to risk bringing it here."

"Who?" she asks, concerned.

"A demon," I reply in a whisper.

Her eyes flare and she furrows her brow, exposing heavy

creases earned with age. "Demons are dangerous," she warns. "Without the guidance of the Coven, you need to stay away."

I lean forward and reach across the table to grab her hand. Deep purple splotches mar her skin, but her touch is soft and familiar. I squeeze it lightly in my own, relishing this moment. I miss her presence at home and her gentle teachings. Without her, I am lost.

"I tried to stay away. I want nothing to do with demons. You taught me enough about their tricks that I know better than to work with them on my own. But, he sent a hellhound after me. It's been stalking me and intimidating me for a while now. That's why I'm here. I need your help."

Slowly, confusion grips her as she watches me. It's as though a fog slides over her mind. Her face slackens slightly, and she shifts in her chair, studying me. I see her memories of me fading away before my eyes. Any hope of a quick resolution fades beside them. A heavy sadness sinks into my stomach, and I let out a quiet sigh.

This happens often these days. Over the last year or so, my grandmother has been slipping into dementia, losing time and misplacing things, and forgetting the people who love her the most. That's why she resides here now. She has been in the assisted care facility for almost three months. Bringing her here broke my heart, but our home isn't safe for her anymore, not with all the occult objects in our possession and her tendency to leave her candles and lit charcoal unattended.

"You need help, darling?" she asks, falling into her comfortable role as a diviner for hire in an attempt to fight away the confusion. For years, she gave tarot readings and read palms from our home. She made quite a name for herself, too. Strangers constantly came and went out of our living room. She always made money to get us by.

Despite her failing mind, my grandmother is, and always

has been, a powerful practitioner. On her foggiest days, even as the most intimate details from her own life have ebbed away, her divination abilities still shine through with the strongest clarity, a fact I am thankful for today. Perhaps I will still receive some of the answers I need, just not in the manner I had intended.

"Who might you be?" she asks with a practiced, kind smile.

I push back the sharp pang of loss and clear my throat, ready to play along.

"My name is Alex," I say, taking on the role of client. "A very powerful entity is tormenting me, and I need your help to send him away. Can you help me?"

"Of course, of course. May I ask what type of entity? There are so many..."

"A demon named Iroth and his hellhound. He wants me to find something for him, but I don't know where to look."

"Iroth? Hmm," she says, trying to search her memory for him and coming up blank. "The name sounds familiar, but I can't quite place it. Let's take a look and see what my cards have to say, shall we?"

I nod, withdrawing my hands and setting them on my lap as she shuffles the cards once more. She carefully chooses three and places them face down before her in a line, flipping them over and studying them one by one.

She begins her reading, squinting at the first card. "There are three cards here. The first represents your recent past. For this, you've been given the Tower. In this position, this card tells me that something significant has recently changed in your life, and not for the better. Have you lost someone close to you, perhaps? A family member or a very close friend?"

"I have," I answer, thinking of the day that I brought her here and the profound sense of loneliness when I returned home to our empty house. "My grandmother recently... departed," I add.

She offers me a sympathetic smile, then returns to her cards. "The loss of someone close to you left you weakened. You've been vulnerable and broken. This demon somehow felt the shift and sought to take advantage of it. They are very crafty like that."

I wait patiently for her to continue, watching her lift the middle card closer to her face.

"The center card represents the present. It tells me what challenges you're currently facing. You've drawn the Nine of Pentacles, undignified. That means upside down," she clarifies as if I do not know tarot myself.

Sadness surges through me at the memory of her practicing with me when I was young, but I shove the memory away. "What does that mean?" I ask, feigning ignorance.

"It means that you are behaving recklessly. Most likely, you're not considering the consequences of your actions because of your intense fear. Demons are indeed terrifying, my child. But, remember this: reckless behavior will get you nowhere. You must think things through before you do them, or you may wind up in far worse trouble than you already are. All actions have consequences," she cautions.

She has no idea how right she is.

My grandmother reaches down and flips the final card, scooping it up and examining it as well.

"This last position represents your near future, and it is the most changeable of all the cards in the spread," she explains, setting it back down and tapping it with her pointer finger. "That's because our futures change with each decision we make. There are millions of potential outcomes. I can only tell you what will come of the path you are pursuing now."

"I understand," I say, waiting for her to interpret the card.

"You've drawn the Ten of Swords," she says, tracing the filigreed blades illustrated on the card. "This is not such a wonderful card in this particular position. This card warns of impending failure and devastation. It is, in my opinion, the least desirable card in the entire deck. Your reading is warning you that whatever you plan to do will cause you more harm than good. You said that this demon wants you to find something for him?" I nod again, watching her closely. "I strongly urge you to reconsider. Whatever he wants, he most certainly should not possess. It is dangerous, and its delivery will cost you dearly."

"I'm afraid that I don't have a choice," I tell her, leaning closer again. "This demon's hound is following me, even now." I glance out the window, but the beast's presence is still concealed. "If I don't find what he is looking for and bring it to him tomorrow before the height of the full moon, he will torture and kill me. He will claim my soul. Please, you have to help me. I've heard from others that you are a powerful practitioner. Can you help me find it?"

My unknowing grandmother sighs and reaches out her hands. I offer her my own, and she squeezes them tightly, closing her eyes in concentration. "What does he want, child? I will try."

"He wants a silver ring," I answer, locking eyes with her across the table. "He claims that it belongs to him and that someone else possesses it. He won't tell me why he wants it back, only that I will die if I fail."

Her eyes shoot open and her mouth turns down into a frown. "I know of the type of ring you are searching for," she answers. "He is a demon of the crossroads, yes?"

"He is," I confirm.

"And you've made a deal with him, haven't you?"

"Not on purpose," I say, ashamed. "He tricked me when I was young and has returned now to call on the debt."

"I see." She sets my hands down on the table and closes her eyes, suddenly weary. "I have worked with a great many demons in my day, child. They possess incredible power which can be used to your advantage if you know how to bend them to your will. But, as I said before, everything comes with a price."

"What do you mean?" I ask, confused.

"Lesser demons did not come across power so great accidentally. They were once human souls that have escaped the torment of eternal punishment by making deals with those even fouler than themselves. These greater demons, princes of damnation, granted them power and eternal life at a cost. Thus, the crossroads demons became creatures of the deal, tricking humans into selling their souls without a true understanding of the cost in much the same way as the greater demons did to the crossroads demons themselves."

I blink in surprise. My grandmother taught me a great many things, but I never learned this. Why did she keep it from me for all these years? It has left me vulnerable and confused. That's not like her at all.

"But, what does this have to do with the ring Iroth is searching for?" I ask, genuinely interested now.

"In transforming the tortured soul, the greater demons must remove the soul's essence from the host. This allows the demons to act with utmost cruelty and no pesky conscience riddling them with guilt and pain. This essence is then trapped inside a physical object, namely a nondescript silver ring. The crossroads demons wear these rings and keep them close because, as all magick has consequences, so does the creation of the talisman. The demon's life is tied to the essence confined inside. Should someone find a way to separate the demon from his ring, it will leave him vulnerable, no longer impervious to injury and death. It ties the bearer to the demon itself, granting the bearer a great advantage that the demon would not wish to share."

"How do you know all of this?" I question. "Surely, demons wouldn't want this information widely known. Wouldn't this secret be kept well hidden?"

"There are things in my past, child, which have made me privy to more information than I should rightfully have access to."

"If someone managed to separate the demon from his ring, what would they do with it?"

"If they were smart," she answers, picking up her cards and returning them to her deck, "they would hide it someplace safe and ward it against the demon itself. Something as valuable as that ring would require many layers of protection, lest the demon find it and reclaim it. I'm certain that the demon would destroy whoever took the ring from him, and possibly anyone close to that person as well."

I nod my head in understanding and ask, "What kind of protection? Would there be some kind of sign?"

"Oh yes, there would be signs. But, to figure out what those may be, you'll need to find the one who separated your demon from his ring and speak with them. This I cannot help you with. I'm sorry, child. I believe our session today has drawn to a close."

Reluctantly, I shake her offered hand and stand, watching her shuffle the deck again and again. She watches me, too. I can see the battle in her mind between the disease and her memories, trying desperately to place my face in her sea of loss.

As I turn to leave, she reaches out her hand and grabs my arm, stopping me. "Have I seen you before?" she asks, studying me again. "You look so familiar. I have a granddaughter around your age, I think. Are you a friend of hers?"

A tear slides down my cheek and I swipe it away. "I'm sorry. You must be mistaken. But, thank you for your help, Ms. Hendricks. I really needed it today."

"Of course, child. Of course. You come back again, alright? I get lonely in here. My granddaughter hasn't come to see me in quite some time. I wonder where she's been," she says, trailing off and staring out the window as if she is searching for me out there behind the glass. Her mind wanders, lost in thought as she struggles to piece the bits of her life back together.

"I'm sure she'll be by soon," I offer, trying to fight back the flood of tears threatening to break free.

"Yes, yes. She will. I know it." She drops my arm and blinks, then looks back up at me, shuffling her cards again. "Can I help you, child? Have you come for a reading?" she asks, having completely forgotten our conversation already.

"No thank you, ma'am," I reply, voice hoarse. "I have to be on my way."

"Alrighty, then. Take care. It looks like rain's coming soon."

"I will," I answer, and I turn and briskly walk away.

Zachariah stands as I pass him. He looks as though he wants to say something, but he stops when he sees the pain on my face. I weave back through the solarium and into the hall, then burst outside into the early autumn air, letting loose the soul-wrenching sob that has been aching inside of me since I sat down beside her.

As I step into my Jeep and fasten the seatbelt, I wonder if Iroth knows how torturous this little adventure was, too. The pocket watch in my shirt ticks loudly, and somehow, I know that he can feel my pain through his stupid enchantment. I throw the car in reverse, back out of my spot, and speed away from the facility as fast as I can, refusing to look back.

CHAPTER SIX

My mind is a whirlwind as I pull into my driveway. Images of my grandmother's vacant eyes staring up at me without recognition haunt me as much as Iroth's impending deadline. I am as helpless to stop the spread of her dementia as I was when faced with the inescapable power that held me in place while the hound mauled me in that old abandoned school.

Worse yet, though I was able to discern why the ring is important to Iroth, I still have no idea how or why my grandmother came into possession of it, and I have absolutely no idea where she may have hidden it.

My time is running short, and the day is slipping away. I have just over thirty hours to locate this ring and deliver it to Iroth or I'll be faced with his depravity once more. Knowing what he did to poor Selena, I'm certain that last night was only a taste of the horrific acts he has planned. I shiver at the thought.

As I approach my front door, the driveway gravel shifts under a heavy weight. The scents of rotting flesh and sulfur return, thick and pungent.

I pause mid-step, turning slowly to search for the figure of the hound, but it is once more concealed in the fading light of day. Of all the powers the beast commands, its ability to become nearly invisible is the most worrisome. I may have a powerful lineage of magick, but even I cannot fight what I cannot see.

Though I can't see the hound, it can most certainly see me. Low, rumbling whispers of my name float toward me on the breeze, taunting and terrorizing me: "Alex. Come play. Alex. Alex."

Quickly, I turn away, bolting toward my house and throwing open the door. I step inside and slam it shut, locking it behind me with a decided click. Safely past the threshold, I lean back against the door, my whole body shaking.

As of yet, the beast has not been able to gain access to our home. Our wardings are too strong. I glance up at the door frame to see one of my grandmother's many protection sachets nailed in place just above it and the series of sigils gouged into the wood. Protection has always been my grandmother's first priority. I only wish that I had taken her lessons closer to heart before foolishly summoning Iroth. If I had, maybe I wouldn't be in this situation.

I press my ear against the door to hear the beast's approach. The hound's long, sharp nails click as it ascends the three steps to the porch. The boards creak beneath its weight. After each heavy footfall, the hound purposefully drags its nails, scratching and scorching the wood.

I hear it pace back and forth outside of the door for several minutes before snorting and retreating down the steps away from the house. In the distance, the few remaining chickens in the coop squawk as it returns to its favorite hideaway. The beast treats the enclosure as a veritable feast, breaking through every lock that I have installed with ease.

I let out a deep breath and force myself away from the threshold, blocking out the awful sounds and walking down the hall to my grandmother's study.

It feels like trespassing as I slide a small bronze skeleton key into the lock on the door and twist. It swings open into the sacred space of its own accord, sending the sweet smell of mint and rose petals out into the hall. The scent reminds me so much of her that my heart skips a beat. Though I know it is impossible, I expect to see her inside, tending to her altar or writing in her grimoire.

This room has always been reserved for the sacred workings of my grandmother's craft. This is where she taught me everything I know about so many rituals, the occult, and my magickal lineage. Without her presence, the space feels vacant and cold. Though by all rights this sacred space should now belong to me, I haven't been able to touch almost anything in it since my grandmother left. As much as I would love to keep her study a shrine in her memory, I no longer have the ability to do so.

I close my eyes and enter the sacred space. Immediately, the power imbued within the room begins to seep into my body and strengthen my essence. The energy is strong, and it tingles like a compressed nerve, but I stand firm until it quiets. I open my eyes, flick on the lights, and look around the room, unsure where to begin.

My grandmother's altar catches my attention. Always lovingly tended to, it now sits in dust-covered neglect. I bow my head as I approach, showing deference to the statuettes of her most revered deities. On the left sits a beautiful bronze replica of Hecate, the woman of three faces, the goddess of witchcraft, the moon, death, and the crossroads. I used to imagine Hecate was a representation of myself, my mother, and my grandmother, as though we three were the maiden, the mother, and the crone. It brought me comfort when I was young and just beginning my journey with the Craft. On the right stands a black statue of Hades, the god of the dead and ruler of the underworld. There have been many other figures honored on the altar during my life, but these two never change. They are our most respected guides and our sacred protectors.

I reach beneath the table and open the top drawer of an apothecary crate to retrieve a dusting cloth and her cleansing spray. I thoroughly dust each item and the surface of the table, returning everything to its place, then spray the altar with Florida Water to remove any negativity that has gathered in its unintentional neglect. I reach back into the crate once more to return the spray and withdraw a few candles and matches. I place the candles next to the statuettes and light them, asking for the divine protection of our deities as I search for and return Iroth's ring. The candles flicker in acceptance of my plea, and I take comfort in knowing that someone is watching over me. I am not entirely alone.

I then move toward the back wall of the study where my grandmother has dutifully cataloged her crystals and herbs and stored her collection of occult items. Many of these items I am familiar with: rose quartz for self-love, tourmaline for protection, mint for prosperity, cinnamon for hastening spell work, her heavy iron ankh talisman, her smooth quartz crystal ball, her assortment of pendulums, and her many tarot and oracle decks. But, for each of the things I have learned about in my time, there are at least two more that I do not understand. In this moment, I am reminded that my grandmother's knowledge is vast. I feel like a child walking in her oversized shoes.

I open what feels like hundreds of small boxes and shake the jars of herbs, listening for a metallic ting against the glass. As expected, after an hour of searching, Iroth's ring is nowhere to be found. It was a long shot, searching for the ring in such an obvious place. It would be unlike her to leave something so dangerous out in the open. But, where would the ring be? I bite my lip as I ponder my next move.

The only thing in this room that I have touched since my grandmother entered assisted living is her grimoire. It sits upon the large wooden desk, pages splayed to the entry regarding summoning a crossroads demon. Her tiny, cramped handwriting sparks a new idea. Throughout my youth, my grandmother was always writing in her soft, leather-bound journals. Perhaps she noted what she had done with the ring in one of them. It's worth a try.

I skirt the desk and squat down by the low bookshelves just beneath the stained glass window. The last dregs of light shine through the colorful depictions of the five elements, casting rainbows up onto the ceiling as I thumb through the shelf's contents and pull several books into my arms. I sigh when I see how many journals there are. I'm a fast reader, but even with my capabilities, this is going to take a while.

I carry the many journals over to the desk and seat myself in her comfortable padded chair. The rainbow cast from the fifth element, spirit, flickers out when the sun sinks below the tops of the trees, and I lean back, trying to summon the energy to get started with this daunting task.

I check my phone to see if my favorite pizza place is still open, and thankfully it is. Before settling down with one of the journals, I place an order, knowing that I won't be able to focus for long unless I eat something. After all, it's been more than twenty-four hours since my last meal.

Order placed, I make myself as comfortable as I can and open the first journal, intruding on my grandmother's private thoughts and memories. It takes nearly an hour before I find the first relevant entry. I read voraciously, stopping only to eat, and fall into my grandmother's story.

January 17th

Corinne has given birth to a healthy baby girl. Though I tried to persuade her to name the baby something more akin to our heritage, she has settled on Alexandria. I must say, it does suit her. She has the biggest dark blue eyes and the chubbiest little cheeks. I will begin stitching her shielding blanket now that I know her name. I can't believe I'm a grandmother! Corinne had no business with that boy, but what a beautiful thing she found in him. I only wish that he had accepted the child instead of running off with that other woman. We will get by just fine, though. We always do.

March 30th

Alexandria has come down with her first illness. I suspect it is the Whooping Cough, and the thought of the poor little thing struggling to breathe terrifies me.

Corinne is an absolute disaster. She has holed herself and Alexandria up in the bathroom near the shower, the hot water turned all the way on high to fill the room with steam. It helps some, but not enough.

The doctors won't do anything for her. I'm going to make an herbal steam sachet with eucalyptus, mint, chamomile, and ginger. May the Mother's blessings help the poor little thing. Tonight, we will hold vigil over her and keep her guard. It's going to be a very tiring evening.

April 2nd

Alexandria's cough has gotten worse. Last night, we had to rush her to the emergency room for a breathing treatment. We spent nearly six hours there, in all. The treatment helped for a short while, but we are now right back to where we started. The steam sachets only provide temporary relief, and the child is too young to withstand any of my healing rituals. I pray to the Mother that she will pull through this. We cannot lose her. She is so very precious. We will hold vigil once more. I must do more research and seek guidance.

April 24th

Our family has not been well.

Corinne is beside herself. Not only have we lost our innocent little baby girl, but I fear that she may be lost to me as well. She wails and weeps when she passes Alexandria's nursery. She won't let me touch her things or make arrangements for the funeral.

I have cast a preservation spell over the poor thing's tiny body, but it will only hold for so long.

I worry that Corinne will do something rash. There are too many hours in the day, and there is only one of me. I cannot watch over her in my sleep, and she vanishes while I am dreaming, only to return many hours later. I do not know where she goes.

I have blessed several stones and asked her to carry them with her just in case she finds herself somewhere she ought not to be. I hope that she listens to me. I cannot bear to lose them both.

SHOCK FLOODS through me as I take in the last entry. I drop my half-eaten slice of pizza back into the box and stare at the words until they blur together. My mind refuses to comprehend what my grandmother has written on the page.

How could I have ever been dead? It makes no sense. I'm sitting here right now, alive. My grandmother is a lot of things, but a necromancer has never been one of them. She couldn't have possibly restored my essence on her own. Not even with the full power of the Coven behind her could she have summoned me back from the hereafter. Besides, if I truly died as an infant, she surely would have told me. An intense feeling of betrayal creeps into my bones as I read further, enthralled.

May 9th

Corinne has ventured off somewhere and has not yet returned home. It's been nearly two days since I saw her last.

At first, I thought she might have returned while I slept, but her bed remains empty and I cannot find her anywhere. I have called the local Sheriff to ask for help, but as she is an adult now and has been gone for less than seventy-two hours, they simply told me that there's nothing they can do.

There is no way I can search these woods on my own. I'm scouring through my books in search of a stronger tracking spell. Perhaps I can track her down that way. I will pray to the Mother for guidance.

May 10th

I found Corinne in the woods in that old abandoned school-house. My tracking spell finally worked once I was able to locate an item with a stronger signature of her essence to guide it.

Though I am thankful she is alive, there is something different about her. She no longer weeps over Alexandria's tiny body. Rather, she looks at her with a determination that I find unsettling.

I wish I could know what she is thinking. Perhaps I can... I will write to the Coven for assistance. Someone must know something that can help me.

May 17th

Corinne has brought great danger upon us all.

Last night, I followed her through the woods, back to the old school house. At first, she was alone. Then, a man appeared and trailed her inside.

I am not ashamed to have eavesdropped through the window. From what I gathered, the man is no man at all, but a crossroads demon. Corinne wants to make a deal with him to bring Alexandria back, but he has yet to name his price.

She will do anything to see it through. I must convince her that this is folly, but I fear my words will fall on deaf ears.

Tonight, I will reinforce my warding. I have conjured a great many demons in my day, but none have ever penetrated these walls. If I can just keep Corinne here and the demons at bay, she will be safe.

I do not know what else to do.

May 20th

I was awoken early this morning by the sounds of an infant's cry. Naturally, I rushed to Alexandria's room. There she was, squirming and rosy-cheeked in her crib.

I feel so many things right now that I don't know what to think. I expected to see Corinne by her side, but she is nowhere to be found once more. All I know is that the deal has been struck.

Corinne is in more danger than she could possibly know. I have learned of this demon's name, and I have never encountered one so deranged in my entire practice.

I pray to the Mother that she has chosen her words carefully. Precise language is key in negotiations with a demon, and I have done my best to protect her from foolish mistakes. Rumor has it that this demon in particular is crafty, a master of language. I fear he will use her desperation against her.

If only she had listened to me.

I will search her out if she isn't home by this evening. I cannot risk exposing Alexandria to the demon directly, so I must wait until I can find someone to watch over her... someone who doesn't know that my poor, innocent little granddaughter has been deceased for nearly a month.

I have to make some calls.

May 22nd

I found her. Corinne is dead.

Whatever deal she struck with that demon, Iroth... it was not worth this. I can't even begin to describe the things that he has done. She doesn't even look like my baby anymore. Her eyes, and her mouth... oh Goddess. A body should not be desecrated like this.

I brought her home this evening, and somehow I must prepare her for the burning. There is so much blood. I can only hope that there is enough of her left to pass on to the hereafter. He has taken so much.

I will make him pay for what he has done to my daughter. The demon Iroth will regret this if it's the last thing I ever do.

December 24

I finally have a plan. It has taken me quite some time and many interrogations to learn of Iroth's weakness: his silver ring.

The last unwitting demon I cornered eventually bent to my will after seeing the remains of his compatriots strewn about in the cavern. Coward. But, he told me what I need to know.

Each crossroad demon is given a silver ring, crafted symbolically from the traitorous coins of Judas, upon their creation. This ring is bound to the demon's eternal soul. Greater demons imbue the ring with enough of the crossroad demon's essence that it separates them from feeling, shielding them from pain and sparing them from mortal injury.

If I can separate the demon Iroth from his ring and somehow bind it to my own essence, I may be able to weaken him enough that I can destroy him. It won't be easy. I have a great deal of research and work to do. I must call upon the Coven once more and prepare the necessary rituals.

I won't rush into this haphazardly as Corinne did. I cannot leave this poor child alone.

March 21st

It is done. I have separated the demon from his ring and tied it to my own essence. Under the guidance of the Coven, I found a way to trick him into trying to barter with me and trapped him.

In the end, I had to sever his finger to gain access to the ring. He is so strong, much stronger than I anticipated. Before my very eyes, his finger regrew with no sign that the injury ever even existed. It was quite a gruesome affair.

I left him there in the cage, but I know that it will not hold one of his strength indefinitely.

As I understand it, the demon is no longer impervious to injury and death because the ritual I acquired from the Coven will force him to age and wither alongside me. He seemed to sense it, too. I have yet to understand what the cost will be for me, but I am no fool. Only time will tell. All magick comes with a price, and this is strong magick, indeed.

He would be foolish to darken our doorstep again. Yet, I remain wary. The demon Iroth knows my name and most likely knows where my family resides. I will need to improve my warding once more.

I only hope that I can continue to protect us both. Alexandria has lost so much already. I cannot let her down.

THERE IS NO MORE mention of Iroth or the ring for quite some time. I furiously flip through page after page, journal after journal, for even the tiniest mention of his name, but I find none until the date indicates that a little over eight years have passed.

I want to look away, knowing that this entry and what follows is because of me, because of what happened to Selena, but I cannot. I force myself to read on.

August 14th

What I have long feared has happened. The demon Iroth has returned. I came home today to find several police cruisers in my drive and a team of paramedics loading my granddaughter's friend onto a stretcher. At first, I was baffled by the scene, but then Alexandria described the incident to me.

Apparently, the demon has been infiltrating her life for weeks. He claims to be a child named Carter, but I know who he is. My poor granddaughter didn't understand what was happening. I should have prepared her for this. She bears so much trauma now. Iroth eviscerated her friend in front of her eyes.

I have brewed a tincture to calm her nerves, and she is resting fitfully. I must gain access to her memories while she sleeps to further study the demon's behavior. I need to protect her from him now more than ever. I have failed her, after all these years. I thought I was a better guardian than this.

I plan to brew a batch of forgetting to dull the memories so that she may lead as close to a normal life as possible, but I have decided. Alexandria will start her training tomorrow. I won't leave her defenseless again.

August 15th

The worst has happened: Just like her mother, Alexandria has made a deal with the demon. I found the bargain buried deep in her memories. She signed her contract in blood in exchange for the return of her friend's life. I'm certain she has no concept of what she has done. The wretched thing has claimed her soul, and it is entirely my fault. If I had only left him alone after Corinne's death, Alexandria might have been spared.

He had to have known who she was. He targets us now out of revenge. But, I've warded us all against him. How could he have found us? I must strengthen my wards once more. Protection is the only thing that matters now. I must keep him away from Alexandria so that he may never call his contract to fruition.

I have a feeling that he has somehow tracked us through his essence in the ring. Tomorrow, I will seek the Coven's guidance once more. They will know how to hide it from him eternally. With our combined magicks, there has to be a way.

August 20th

It is done. I have constructed a box of wrought iron and filled it with the necessary salts and herbs. This, I have sealed, encased in cedar, and buried deep beneath the sacred tower. Unless someone knows where to find it, it will not likely be discovered.

The ring must never be returned to Iroth. He must be forced to wither and age as he so deserves. Let this be the end of this hell. So mote it be.

I FLASH BACK through many lessons with my grandmother, desperately trying to remember a mention of the sacred tower. There's something... a vague thought in my mind that I can't quite access. Try as I may to conjure it, it shrouds itself and retreats from me.

My eyes water from exhaustion and strain to focus on the journals. The flickering candles on the altar have long since extinguished themselves, leaving the room dim. My concentration has grown weak.

I catch myself drifting off to sleep when the stack of journals slips from my lap and lands with a series of thumps on the floor. Reluctantly giving in to my body's need for rest, I bend down and scoop up the journals, placing them in a neat pile atop the desk, but a smattering of pages have fallen loose and onto the floor. A final page catches my eye.

June

I do not know the date today. Things are slipping away from me so often now. I don't even feel like myself. I can feel my mind fading. I knew that this day would come. All magick comes with a price. My daughter made a deal for Alexandria's life, and Alexandria made a deal for that little girl, Selena. I suppose when I performed the ritual many years ago, I made a deal of my own.

The cost of weakening Iroth is weakening myself. I have damaged my mind, and there is no way to fix what has been broken. My only comfort is that when I lose myself, Iroth must also lose himself. Alexandria will truly be safe then. I will happily endure this for her, and for my sweet daughter Corinne who was taken from us far too soon.

I only hope that someday, Alexandria finds these journals and understands what we have done. I have never told her of her death and resurrection for fear of further traumatizing her poor soul.

But Alexandria, if you're reading this, you must know this one thing. Iroth must never be reunited with his ring. If he is, all of this will have been in vain.

I'm counting on you now. Hold the line. Remain strong. Our ancestors are with you. I have taught you all that I can. I only wish that we had more time. I love you, sweet girl. Be safe.

Blood drains from my face as I hold the loose page close to my chest. Clearly, my grandmother knew exactly what was happening to her all this time, but she never told me a thing. How could she keep so many secrets?

I could have tried to help her. We could have worked together to restore her mind. She simply gave in to the decline in order to achieve her goals! She has willingly left me behind, and now I must face Iroth alone.

I sob, staring down at the paper in my hands.

I have lost everyone that I've ever loved. Is there even a point in finding the ring anymore? What do I have left to live for?

I storm out of the room, flicking off the lights and slamming the door irreverently. A small part of me feels that the height of the full moon can't come fast enough. If I die at Iroth's hands, knowing now that he is responsible for what little life I have lived, it will only be a completion of the mess my mother started in the first place. The thought strikes me as almost karmic.

This night has grown long, and it's too late for me to care. Morning will be here soon.

I hate playing this stupid game. She should have left me for dead.

CHAPTER SEVEN

I sleep fitfully, tossing and turning through vivid nightmares. Scenes from my grandmother's journal play behind my shuttered eyes.

My mother wails over my infant corpse and she holds my limp little body tight to her chest. Her agony radiates through me as she rocks back and forth, refusing to allow my grandmother to take me from her.

The dream flashes to my mother manically digging up the dirt at the crossroads with her bare hands. Her fingernails split as she displaces the hard-packed earth, and the tips of her fingers begin to bleed, but she keeps going. She plants a small box, much like my own, into the ground and buries it. Her eyes are wide with anticipation as she waits.

Iroth materializes and approaches her from behind. He possesses a different form, but his movements and menacing grin are entirely his own. I'm powerless to stop him as he grabs ahold of my mother's neck from behind and jerks her up off of the ground, turning her to face him. His pointed nails pierce her skin, but she doesn't care. She shamelessly begs him to make a deal with her in exchange for my life. He sneers and laughs mercilessly, but he doesn't respond.

Again, the dream shifts, this time to my grandmother lifting my mother's mangled body into the bed of her old pickup. Her hands are drenched in blood, and it smears across her face when she wipes away the sweat on her brow. She hesitates before driving the truck home, staring at what remains of her daughter with utterly haunted eyes.

My grandmother places my mother's linen-wrapped body, prepared for the final rite, onto the funeral pyre with such loving devotion that my heart breaks for her. She ignites the tinder and retreats to the edge of the ritual circle, joining the other members of the Coven as the flames eat their way through my mother's lifeless flesh.

She reaches for me, and another practitioner passes me over to her. My infant self squirms in my grandmother's grasp, uncomprehending. Through her tears, she smiles down at me comfortingly and pulls me close.

When my alarm sounds at seven am, I wake less rested than I had been the night before.

I'm drenched in sticky sweat and my throat feels raw from crying out to my family in my sleep. Every muscle in my body resists as I sit up and peel back the sheets, rising clumsily to my feet. My pajamas cling to me uncomfortably. Like a zombie, I drag myself through the hall and into the bathroom for a cold shower.

My eyes are still weighted with lead as I step out and scramble to find warmth in my jeans. I inspect the hound's mark and am relieved that at the very least, the burns seem to be healing well. The pain has lessened into an annoyance more so than a continual, searing heat. I once again coat it with salve and cover it with fresh gauze before slipping into my shirt and heading downstairs for nature's best cure for a long night: coffee.

The slow dripping of the coffee is torturous, but by the time the pot is finished, the smell of the strong brew manages to awaken my senses. I slam two cups before allowing myself to sit down at the kitchen table and formulate a plan.

Today is my last chance. I have to find the ring or there won't be anything left of me by morning.

Worse yet, I have to decide what to do with it. My grandmother's journals were very clear: Iroth must never be reunited with his ring. But, if I don't return it to him by tonight's full moon, he has made it abundantly clear that the consequence will be my slow, torturous death. I find this outcome incredibly undesirable, and I can't help but feel that if Iroth is allowed to mutilate and murder me, my mother will have died in vain.

She made that deal eighteen years ago to save my life, and it would be cruel to simply accept my fate and throw it all away.

Neither option, keeping the ring from him or returning it to him, feels like the correct solution. I'm torn between two different wrongs with no clear middle ground.

My grandmother will be of no help in this situation. She can't instruct me on how best to protect myself any longer. Her mind is too far gone. Whatever I decide, this decision falls on me alone, and the thought of doing this alone is absolutely terrifying.

I feel a vibration inside the pocket of my jeans and reach down. My hand skims across a lump, almost perfectly round. Iroth's pocket watch. A dry laugh escapes me as I retrieve the watch and open the casing.

The watch's face glows a faint red as the hands tick away the time. I know for certain that I did not put this watch in my pocket this morning, yet nothing about this showy little trick surprises me. It is a reminder, once more, that I am running out of time, meant specifically to induce panic. I close the casing and return it to my pocket, hooking the chain around my belt loop.

"Yeah, I get it," I say to no one in particular. "I'm working on it, you jackass."

The watch vibrates again, almost disapprovingly. I roll my eyes and ignore it.

Instead of acknowledging Iroth's taunt, I pour myself a bowl of cereal and carry it back to my seat. I'm not hungry, but I know that I should eat. Most likely, I have a long day ahead. I pick at it, pushing it around in my bowl and staring reluctantly across the hall at the closed door to my grandmother's study.

I don't want to go into that room again. In fact, it's one of the last places I want to be. I had not been ready for the revelations I found inside my grandmother's journals. Try as I might to avoid learning more horrific things about my past, I know that her study may be the only place with the information I need regarding the ring's whereabouts. I'll have to go back inside.

I still can't recall anything meaningful about whatever the sacred tower is. The words feel so familiar, but the information is hovering just out of my reach. I'm certain that my grandmother must have taught me about whatever it is in my lessons, or maybe she has even taken me to wherever it is before. The nagging sense of familiarity scratches at my mind as I deposit the cereal bowl into the sink.

Giving in, I slip the small brass key back into the lock on the study door and allow the door to swing wide. I step inside the sacred space and endure the tingling surge of power before returning to the altar space.

Like yesterday, I place new candles on the altar and light them, asking for protection and guidance from Hecate and

Hades in hopes that it might help me find what I need before my time runs out. I'm struck with the sudden realization that both of these deities are related to crossings as I toss the burnt match into the little dish on the side.

I wonder if, all this time, that's the reason my grandmother has called upon the two of them. I chastise myself for being blind to so many things. I should have been paying more attention. I have been so very foolish.

This time, I add an offering of dragon's blood incense to the center of the altar, too. I watch as the fragrant smoke spirals to the ceiling, indicating an acceptance of my offering, for which I am incredibly thankful. I send up a silent prayer, asking the deities to stay with me today. With the deities on my side, perhaps I'll stand a better chance of survival tonight. I thank them for their presence before returning to my task.

I pick up another of my grandmother's journals in search of more information about Iroth's ring. Though there are hundreds of entries, frustratingly, my search yields nothing new. After almost two hours, I return the journals to the shelf under the window and scan the room for anything else that may be of use.

I think back to all of the occult reference books I had been assigned to read during my earliest studies of the Craft. Using the desk chair to climb, I retrieve them all one by one and set them on the desk. Diligently, I flip through them, searching the indices for any mentions of sacred towers.

I find what I am looking for inside a particularly thick tome. After reading through the designated chapter on creating natural altar spaces, I learn that sacred towers are essentially natural altars, constructed in a place of power in the wilderness that can also be carefully concealed from others. These towers allow practitioners to enhance their spells and rituals by harnessing the five elements of the Craft: Earth, Air, Water, Fire, and Spirit.

Exasperated, I slam the book closed and lean my head into my hands. I know what the sacred tower is now, but how am I supposed to find yet another thing that has been intentionally concealed from me?

Abandoning the reference books, my eyes fall upon my grandmother's grimoire. For years, she has been cataloging her practices within its pages. I shove the textbooks away and gingerly lift the heavy heirloom from its stand on the desk. The binding creaks and the thick, aged pages crackle as I flip through them. If my grandmother recorded any information about her sacred tower and Iroth's ring, the only place she would have done so is within these pages.

Page after page reveals nothing, not even a mention of a tower or a spell-casting site away from our home. I turn the very last page and sigh, completely crushed.

This is it. This is the last place I know to look. She wouldn't keep any information about her magick outside of this room, especially not something as important as this. She would have guarded it and sealed it away somewhere no one would think to look, but somewhere that still made sense and would be easily accessible to her.

Something about the idea of "sealing the information away" gives me an idea. A tiny sliver of hope bursts through me. What if... what if it *is* here? What if it *is* inside this book after all?

I search the spine first, feeling for notches or raised edges in which a page may have been hidden.

There is nothing there, so I give the thin purple ribbon marker a tug. It holds firm.

Next, I feel inside the front cover of the text, sliding my

fingers along the seams and over the thin pastedown in search of lumps. The front cover yields nothing, but the back...

In the center of the pastedown, there is an ever-so-slightly raised ridge. I rip open the top desk drawer and snatch up her sword-shaped letter opener, carefully lifting the edges to damage the heirloom as little as possible, until the pastedown comes away with ease. A single sheet of paper slips free, falling to the surface of the desk. I nearly drop the grimoire in surprise as I hastily pick up the page, reading its contents.

Alexandria,

I knew that you would find this letter someday. There can only be one reason why you have sought out this information — the demon Iroth has returned.

I am sorry that I was not able to protect you from him, but the magick I have used to separate him from his essence has cost me dearly. The strain of maintaining the bond between his essence and my own is draining my mind. As I have taught you, magick always comes with a price. I will happily pay this one if it means that I can render Iroth mortal, as he will become at the time of my passing. It is the only way that I know to destroy him. We cannot allow him to survive.

By now, I expect he has called in the favor extorted from the pact you made with him so many years ago. My assumption is that he has tasked you with recovering his silver ring. This is something I urge you not to do.

Iroth is more dangerous than you could ever know. If you only knew what he did to your mother, you would understand what this wicked demon is truly capable of. I know you remember what he did to little Selena. He has done many worse things in his time. He is old, Alexandria. He has committed atrocities that laid entire cities to waste. He cannot be allowed to do this any longer. We must make him pay for his crimes.

I know that he has made you promises of salvation in return for fulfilling your contract. Demons always do. But, you must know this: he will say or do anything to be reunited with his essence. Should he regain control of it once more, he will not spare you. He may release you from your deal, but his thirst for vengeance will not be satisfied. He may not be able to claim your soul, but I am certain that you will end up like your mother.

There is no easy way out of a devil's bargain. Returning the ring to Iroth will only break our bond and free him from his torment, granting him full control of his power once more.

Mother help you, Alexandria. You must endure through the fear of death and face him with courage, even if it means the end of your days and mine.

I wish that I could take the burden of this task from you, but by the time you find this letter, all that will remain of my knowledge of the Craft will be here inside of my grimoire. I have spent years teaching you to control your magick. Draw from my teachings and harness your strength now.

Retrieve the cast iron box from beneath the sacred tower I built in the old mining tunnels, and use the instructions on the back of this letter to guide you in the construction of your own. Harness the power of the elements to build up the necessary wards once more, for as my time here draws to an end, my own wards will slip and fail.

He will be able to find the ring when I am gone. Stop him, Alexandria. I know that you can. Force him to pay for all that he has done, and avenge all those to whom he has brought harm.

Know that I love you, my child. Your mother loves you too, though she cannot be here to tell you so. Blessed be, and remain strong in the knowledge that the two of us will stand beside you in spirit, no matter what happens now.

Your Grandmother,
Elizabeth Hendricks

ON THE BACK of the letter in her cramped handwriting, I find explicit details regarding how my grandmother built her own sacred tower with the expert guidance of the Coven. Painstakingly, she describes ideal locations for gathering energy, the chants and prayers she used to manifest her intentions, the specific runes and talismans that can be used to most effectively enhance strong magickal wards, and materials most suitable for the protection of a powerful occult object like Iroth's ring of essence.

I'm awed by the knowledge and power my grandmother has secretly wielded and the strength it must have taken to keep Iroth at bay. I've never seen a ritual as complex as this in all my years of practicing the Craft. After all of the training my grandmother has given me, and even with the specificity of the instructions written here, I have no idea if I am capable of following in her footsteps. If I do this, it will be the most complicated magickal undertaking I've ever attempted. Even if I can pull this off, I have no idea if there will be enough time.

At least I know where to find the ring. That gives me a starting point for whatever must come next. I place the page of instructions inside the front cover of my grandmother's grimoire, then wrap the heirloom in an extra altar cloth for protection. Retrieving a large satchel, I delicately place the grimoire in the bag. I rummage through my grandmother's spell ingredients, placing jar after jar of the suggested items into the satchel alongside the grimoire. I even borrow a few extra items for my personal protection: another necklace, a veil, and a bottle of holy water. I clasp the necklace alongside my own, tie the veil in place on my head, and tuck the holy water into my pocket for quick access, just in case I need it in a pinch.

Satisfied that I have followed my grandmother's instructions, I lace myself into a pair of old hiking boots and grab my thick canvas jacket. My journey to the abandoned mine will lead me through some of the densest patches of the woods, and the terrain will be treacherous. I'm certain Iroth's hound will be right at my heels, and I can't afford to move slowly enough to avoid the sharp outcroppings, low-hanging branches, and thorny brambles.

I cover every possible inch of my skin and move as quietly as I can to the back door.

I slide the curtain away from the door's small glass window and peer outside, searching for the hound. I can't see the beast, but something tells me that it's there, waiting.

With one last deep breath, I summon up my courage. I burst out of the door and race toward the woods behind my home, running at top speed and praying that the deities are with me after all.

CHAPTER EIGHT

I MANAGE TO DASH HALFWAY ACROSS THE OPEN FIELD BEFORE snagging the attention of the hound. It must have been in the chicken coop again, as startled squawks ring out from behind me. I turn my head to see the door to the coop fly off its hinges. I still can't see the beast, but I hear its heavy footfalls thudding with each bound.

I need to clear the forest's edge before the beast reaches me. It's incredibly fast, much faster than I could ever hope to be. The weight of the satchel slows me down. It bounces off of my back as I surge forward. My muscles burn with the exertion of running across the uneven terrain.

As I near the forest's edge, the atrocious scent of the beast permeates the air. I cringe, but I don't turn back to look again. Without hesitation, I plunge into the dark woods, ducking under the larger branches of the outer trees and propelling myself over jutting roots and through dense weeds. There used to be a path here, but it has long since overgrown. Selena and I played in these woods, years ago. I know the way to the tunnels by heart. I just have to get there in time.

The thorny brambles tug at my jacket and jeans like little hands, and the thinner branches whip across my face as I power through the brush.

I veer to the right and cut through the thicket of bushes where my grandmother and I used to forage for fresh blackberries. The creature may be faster than me, but it is also larger and less agile. If the brambles slow my pace, I'm certain that they will slow the hound's pace as well. I crush sweet berries beneath my feet as I move swiftly through them, hearing branches behind me snap under the weight of the hound.

I barrel out of the thicket and nearly crash into a tree, but I manage to grab the trunk instead and quickly orient myself. Clinging to it, I catch my breath. Going straight is the fastest path to the tunnels. I could keep running for about a half mile, but my legs are starting to feel weak and my chest is burning. I don't know if I'll be able to make it there unscathed.

But, the creek running beneath the old bridge by the schoolhouse cuts through these woods as well. It's just ahead to the left, and the hound hates running water. It would mean a longer distance, but if I sacrifice my speed, I might be able to hold the hound at bay long enough to cross the creek and cut through the rest of the woods safely without straining myself into a complete collapse.

Thinking fast, I shove my body away from the oak tree and head left toward the creek. The hound bellows not far behind, quickly gaining on me now that it too has escaped the tangles of the blackberry patch.

I hear the water first, and hope swells within me. I grab the straps and pull my satchel closer to my back to keep the weight of it centered for balance.

As the creek grows nearer, my boots begin to slide through the moistening undergrowth with each hurried step. I urge my legs to move faster, and for a moment I pick up speed, but I quickly lose my balance and slip, falling to my hands and knees just before the dense plant life gives way to the muddy creek bank.

I scramble to right myself, but before I can fully rise, the hound is upon me. A hot burst of steam overtakes me and the beast slams into my back, knocking me once more to the earth. I kick wildly, trying desperately to fend off the creature, but it catches one of my boots in its maw and tugs me away from the creek and back into the cover of the trees.

I roar at the beast, summoning all of my strength as I kick out with my other foot again and again. One hard blow strikes the hound's invisible form and it snarls, dropping my booted foot to the ground. I watch in horror as the creature begins to materialize in front of my eyes.

Thick, black streams of smoke coalesce into its hulking, grotesque body. I shove myself backward with my boots, unable to stand. Hungry, burning, red eyes glare at me as it lowers its head to the ground and slowly stalks toward me.

Only then do I remember the flask of holy water in my pocket.

Before the hound can pounce on me once more, I grab a hold of the glass flask and use my mouth to rip off the cork stopper. I spit this directly at the hound's face, and it flinches, giving me just enough time to bring the flask up and fling the water at the creature.

On contact, the water sizzles and sputters, inciting enough pain that the hound whimpers and backs away several paces. I fling the flask toward it again, dousing the creature once more. The hound howls and backs away farther, shaking its enormous head in a futile attempt to remove the offending spray.

With the creature distracted, I rise to my feet and pivot away, dashing headlong for the water's edge. The hound races behind me, snapping and swiping at me, but I remain just out of reach.

My boots splash as I enter the creek. Cold water rushes up my legs, and I lift the satchel above my head as I cross to the other side. I turn to see the hound glaring at me. Thick foam drips from its open mouth as it snaps its sharp teeth in my direction. My whole body shakes. I stare back at it and clutch my side, trying to force an intense cramp to release.

I've bought myself some time. Now, I have to put it to good use.

I will myself back into motion, trudging through the edge of the trees and on to the tunnels. I skirt large piles of rocks and avoid the overgrowth, using the trees to propel myself forward, but I'm running on fumes. I don't know how long the creek will deter the hound, but if I don't move faster, it won't matter anyway.

Finally, I see the boarded-up entrance to the mine set into the rocky edge of a foothill just ahead. I pant as I force myself to cross the last twenty or so feet. As I reach the threshold, I practically collapse, unable to hold myself up any longer with my trembling legs.

I'm far from safe, and I know that, but I've made it this far. I lean my head back against the boards and send up a silent plea to the deities for their aid, breathing in as deeply as my throbbing chest will allow.

Far too soon, I hear a deafening crash in the distance as the hound bursts through the tree line, sprinting straight toward me. I use the boards to pull myself shakily to my feet and begin the process of ripping them away from the entrance.

It will take more time than I have to spare to remove enough of them to allow myself access to the tunnels, so I make a quick decision. I hold firm to the nail-riddled board in my hands and stand my ground, turning to face the hound as it draws near.

With all the strength I have left, I swing the board at the creature. It collides with the hound's thick snout with a sickening crack. The beast roars, and I bring the board back down on it again, this time drawing blood. It staggers back once more and paws at its face, knocking away the nails that have pierced the creature's flesh.

As the hound tends to its wounds, I kick my way through the remaining boards until I've created a large enough space near the bottom for my body to slip inside.

I remove my satchel and toss it through safely. Then, flattening myself against the ground, I reach through the gap and shove my arm in first, only to be met with excruciating pain.

The familiar tingling pulse from my grandmother's sacred space zips up my arm, only it's amplified, so strong that it physically repels me from the ward. I gape at my hand as it swells, ballooning just as my foot had when I accidentally stepped on a wasp as a child.

Of course she would ward this space. My panic caused me to behave irrationally, just as I had in summoning Iroth. No one in their right mind would leave a powerful occult object unguarded. But, how is it warded? I see no runes or stones, no talismans or herbs. It has to be something else, something stronger.

My mind races, casting itself back through my studies as quickly as it can, but in my distraction, I lose track of the hound. It isn't until the beast's sour sewage breath warms my face that I look up, realizing my mistake.

I try to back away, but the hound raises its enormous paw and swipes it across my back, slicing through my canvas jacket like it isn't even there and raking its claws against my skin, leaving deep gashes.

I scream in agony and roll away, leaving smeared blood on the grass beneath me.

The hound tilts its head to the side, tauntingly watching and waiting. I reach around to gingerly touch my fingers to my wounds and pull back a glistening, bloody hand.

Blood. She warded the tunnels with blood. I need to get to that entrance, now.

I struggle to my feet, wincing with every movement. As I rise, the beast hunches down low to the ground, muscles tense and ready for pursuit. In this moment, I realize that the hound doesn't just want to fulfill Iroth's orders. It wants the thrill of the hunt. I am the prey, and it is the predator. The hound bares its sharp fangs and licks its lips hungrily.

I only have one shot at this. I have to make this count.

As if in surrender, I throw my hands in the air. Incredibly slowly, I sidestep away from the hound, retreating back to the forest. The beast turns its body to face me and takes two shallow steps, mirroring my movements. I take a deep breath and tense, ready to run.

Concentrating as hard as I can, I count down in my head.

Five... another breath.

Four... wiggle my feet slightly to check my grip on the grass below.

Three... flex my fingers.

Two... a furtive glance behind me to the trees.

One... another deep breath.

Run.

I dig my feet into the ground with every bit of strength I possess and dart back toward the trees, hearing the hound launch itself after me in chase. Just as the beast is about to lunge for me, I drop, causing it to leap over my head. It digs its deadly claws into the ground, slowly skidding to a stop, leaving the beast closer to the tree line and me closer to the entrance to the mine.

I pivot, once more digging into the earth and propelling myself forward, legs moving faster than they ever have before. I pray to the Mother that my years of softball are as useful to me now as the magic my grandmother has taught me to control. Less than three feet from the entrance, I lean into a rapid slide, letting my entire bloody backside slip across the grass and through the small gap that had repelled me so completely only minutes before.

The grass beneath me disappears, replaced by bits of jagged stone and hard-packed dirt. My wounds throb from the force of the slide and I gasp at the pain. I dig my fingers into the scree to slow myself, and when I stop, I force myself onto my side, tears streaming down my face onto the dirt below.

I brace myself for the same shocking pain as before, but it doesn't come. Rolling to my stomach, I tip up my head and gawk at the entrance in disbelief. I really did it! I didn't die! I made it inside the mine!

Furious to be deprived of its meal, the hound paces back and forth outside the entrance, unable to follow me through the gap. It snorts and yowls, slashing and biting angrily at the remainder of the wooden boards.

With shaking hands, I reach out and retrieve my satchel, clutching it close to my chest like a shield. My heart pounds like a sledgehammer. I wait for it to slow, for my breathing to calm, before pushing myself off the ground with tremendous effort and turning my back to the entrance. Before me, the dark tunnel leads deep into the hillside, splitting in several directions, then burrowing down into the earth. I retrieve an old flashlight from the satchel and turn it on, pointing the light down the path and into the dark where somewhere far inside the mine, my grandmother's sacred tower lies in wait.

CHAPTER NINE

Several hours later, the heavy footfalls of the pacing hound sound just outside as I near the boarded threshold, the only entrance or exit to the tunnel.

I crouch down to peer through the gap near the bottom, only to be confronted with glowing red eyes and a snarling mouth full of lethal teeth. The hound growls deeply and swipes at the remaining boards, trying to reach through the gap to me, but the wards are still holding firm — for now.

I stand and withdraw the surprisingly plain silver ring from my pocket and slip it onto my thumb, feeling my skin sizzle beneath the band as it settles in place. I grit my teeth until the pain ebbs. The smell of my own burnt flesh wafts up, and I cringe.

My nagging conscience reminds me that this is not what my grandmother has asked me to do. She wants me to protect the ring and hide, maybe for the rest of my life, so that Iroth might someday accidentally meet his fate and I might find some semblance of safety.

I considered it. I truly did, but with Iroth's deadline looming, I do not have enough time to build such a complex structure as a sacred tower. At least, that's what I've told myself. More importantly, I do not want to spend the rest of my life in hiding. I want to avenge my mother's death. I want to make Iroth pay for my grandmother's ruined mind. I want to show him that I'm not a helpless little chew toy he can toss to his hound.

I refuse to back down. And so, I will follow my own plan, no matter what it takes.

In any case, I doubt that I could remove the ring now, even if I wanted to. If Iroth wants this ring, he'll have to take the whole finger with it. Of course, I doubt that would bother him much at all.

My thumb throbs as I feel his essence roiling just beneath the silver's surface. Alongside it, a softer essence, that of my grandmother, wars with Iroth's will, keeping it in check. When I close my eyes, I can almost see the two essences colliding, oil on water in a prison of smoke and metal. It brings me comfort that my grandmother is truly here beside me, even though I know what I must now do.

I reach into the satchel and retrieve my grandmother's athame, tucking it into my pocket. Its sheath clinks against Iroth's ridiculous watch as the knife settles to the bottom. The blade is sharp, honed to direct magick at the user's will. In a physical confrontation, it will come in handy.

I check the flask of holy water, but only a few drops remain. Wishing I had the foresight to bring more with me, I toss the useless glass container aside. The rest of the satchel I leave behind. I don't have much use for the other things inside now, and the last thing I need is for Iroth to get his hands on my grandmother's grimoire. Goddess only knows what he could do with access to the information that she and our Coven have learned through generations of careful study.

I place the satchel reverently in the corner with a promise to return as soon as I can and restore the heirloom to its proper place.

Guilt washes over me as I lower myself down to the tunnel floor and slide toward the exit, moving slowly in an attempt not to provoke the hound any further. As I near, its sharp claws dig into the earth outside, leaving gouges in the dirt as it postures threateningly.

"I have Iroth's ring," I announce, bringing my face close to a smaller section of the gap.

The hound snaps its foaming mouth at me but lowers its head down to the ground.

"If you want me to give it to him, you have to let me out of this tunnel. He will never get his hands on it if I die in here. I promise you that."

The hound snorts, eyeing me carefully. I hear it whisper my name in that same frightening way, "Alex. Alex comes out to play. Alex."

"I'm not going to play with you," I state firmly. "The sun is gone, and Iroth wants this ring. I need to get to that crossroads now. Do you understand? You let me out of this tunnel or Iroth will know that you failed. I wonder, what does he do to beasts that don't follow his commands?"

The beast snorts and hot steam shoots from its nostrils, bouncing off the invisible force of the wards. It eyes me hatefully before stepping back several paces, poised to pounce, but granting me enough access to slide through the gap and into the dark of the night.

I stare at the hound for a moment, waiting for any signs that it will attack as I escape, but it simply stands there, eerily still, waiting. I lay flat on my stomach, slowly using my hands and arms to creep through the gap and into the cool night air. The creature watches me closely, head cocked to the side.

When I am able to pull the last of myself through, I rise and wipe the dirt and dust off of my jacket and jeans, coughing. The hound shows no signs of an impending attack, so standing very still, breath caught in my throat, I allow the beast to approach me.

It sniffs me aggressively and knocks its enormous, spiky body into my own, sending me stumbling back, off balance. My heart pounds, but I make no move to run. It sniffs me again, this time licking the back of my jacket where the blood from my earlier wounds has seeped through.

I swallow, but the beast backs down and turns away. It casts one last glance in my direction, confusion clear in its uncertain gestures, then begins a slow trot toward the trees and the path that will lead us through the woods to the cross-roads where its master awaits.

The path through the woods is more treacherous at night. I trip over raised roots and find myself snagged on brambles and branches often as I follow the hound. It takes the long way around, avoiding the creek and approaching the old school-house from behind. As a particularly thick branch slams into my chest, I curse and chastise myself for leaving my flashlight behind. I could swear I hear the beast chuckle in amusement at my pain.

It feels like an hour before the sounds of the crickets and frogs dissipate and we break through the boundary of the trees. Just ahead, the old schoolhouse looms like an omen, casting a deep, dark shadow in the bright light of the moon.

The hound slows its pace, falling behind me and growling, shoving me forward with its snout. I shoot it a loathsome look but keep moving, rounding the corners of the building until I can see the large space where the doors once stood and the vile figure leaning against the frame.

He is in a fresh suit this evening, a deep black jacket with pinstripes layered over a crisp white shirt and a charcoal vest. He tugs his white cuffs down past his jacket sleeves and straightens himself, turning to face the hound and me. Without a word, he raises one wrist as if checking the time, tapping the space where a watch should be, then looks up to the perfectly spherical moon above.

"Punctual," he offers, clearly annoyed. "I did say to be here by the height of the full moon, and it appears that you have taken me quite literally, Alex. I don't like to be kept waiting."

"Missing something?" I ask, voice dripping with sarcasm. "A watch, perhaps? I believe I have one of yours. Let me see..." I reach into my pocket and retrieve the pocket watch, tossing it disdainfully at his feet. "Nice touch."

"Yes, yes. I thought it was just the thing!" he responds with a smirk, awfully pleased with himself. He extends his hand and the pocket watch flies straight into his open palm. Smugly, Iroth clasps the chain to his jacket and tucks the watch into his vest pocket, patting it.

"The newspapers were a lovely addition, a little reminder of the mess I caused when I was young."

"Just something special for you, Pet. I hope you liked them. Did you? Did your heart just burst when you saw that I procured them for you?"

"Hardly," I answer. "But you knew that already. You knew I would destroy them. That little enchantment you cast certainly caught me off guard when I threw them into the fireplace. I should have expected theatrics from you. Even as Carter, you always enjoyed a good show."

He chuckles, then extends his hand to me, waiting for me to allow him to usher me inside. I refuse, walking around him defiantly into the building, leaving him standing at the entrance and staring after me.

"Come now, that was simply unpleasant behavior. I'm

disappointed, Alex. I have been looking forward to our reunion for two entire days, and you snub me like I have some sort of infectious disease. I was only offering you my hand."

"I'll take nothing from you," I spit, righting a desk and slipping inside.

Iroth follows suit, sitting directly across from me, just as he had before.

"Déjà vu," he jokes, leaning back into the seat. "History does have a way of repeating itself. Tell me, will there be any more repeat performances tonight? I would hate to watch another young Hendricks witch die on this rotting floor."

Recognizing his taunt for what it is, I refuse to give him a reaction. Instead, I stare at him, locking eyes with the predator before me.

He frowns, disappointed in my lack of response. "Tell me, where is my ring, Alex?" he demands.

I cross my arms over my chest, drawing his attention to my hands. "What, this ring?" I ask, sneaking in a taunt of my own. "It took me quite some time to find it. Now that I have, I've grown fond of it. I may just keep it for myself. Don't you think it looks great on me?" I inspect my thumb, turning my hand so I can view the ring from all angles. "I've become quite... attached to it, as you can see."

Iroth narrows his eyes into deadly slits and leans forward over the little wooden desk, propping his face up on his hands. "Indeed. It appears that you have."

"I learned quite a few things about this ring over the last couple of days. Did you know that crossroads demons are given rings like these to contain bits of their own essence? I didn't know that. You learn something new every day."

"Are they?" he asks, feigning innocence. "How intriguing."

"Yes, it really is. And did you know that if a powerful witch wants to, she can bind a demon's essence to her own, forcing it into a slow decline to mortality as the witch ages and fades? I found that piece of information absolutely fascinating. What a novel concept."

"Mmm," he answers through gritted teeth. "Go on, Pet. What else do you know?"

"Well, I know that this particular ring belongs to you, and I know that my grandmother performed exactly such a ritual many, many years ago after you murdered my mother and left her mangled corpse for my grandmother to find."

"Did she?" he spits, voice full of venom. "It seems like you have done quite a bit of research, Alexandria. But, do you know the old saying, Pet? Curiosity killed the cat. I'd tread lightly if I were you. You have no idea the rules of the game that you are playing."

"Rules?" I ask, projecting more calm than I feel. "I'm afraid you don't know the rules, Iroth. How silly of you to assume I would play along with your scheme."

Iroth abruptly stands, shoving his desk across the room and storming over to me. Reaching me, he bends down, slamming his hands into my desk and curling his fingers around the edges, lowering his face to my own. His long fingers grip the edge of the desktop so tightly that the wood groans from the pressure. "Alexandria, hand over my ring, now. I will not warn you again."

"No," I answer defiantly. "I don't think I will."

"We have a contract!" he roars, face purpling with rage. "You will hand over my ring or I will end your life and drag your soul from your bleeding corpse. This is your last chance!"

Anger surges through me, a kind of rage I have never before felt. I rise to my feet, forcing Iroth to stand, as I say, "Like you did to my mother? What did you do to her, Iroth?"

My confidence shakes him, and his eyes search my face,

looking for a hint of weakness. He growls, and the hound's ears lift to attention as it watches us bicker across the room.

"Very well," he says. "If you truly must know, I'll tell you every last detail. Settle in, Pet. This may take a while."

Like before, red streams of magick rush out from beneath his sleeves, shoving me backward. My boots screech as I fight to resist the pressure sliding me across the floor and fail. The old slate board slams into my back as my body reaches the far wall, sending a sharp pain through the hound's gashes and knocking the air from my lungs. I gasp as the tendrils wrap themselves around my neck and my wrists, squeezing so tightly I feel blood pool in my face and hands.

"Your mother came to me to bargain for your little infant life, as I'm sure you well know."

Iroth stalks toward me, extending his hands out and flexing his long fingers. He lets his perfectly human projection begin to dissipate, showing glimpses of his true self hiding just beneath the surface. The flesh of his face has been burned away, leaving large areas of exposed muscle and tendon. His sharp black nails begin to grow, forming long, honed talons at the tips of his hands.

"And I, being such the indulgent humanitarian as I am, acquiesced. I drew your tiny, squirming soul back from the hereafter into your little corpse." He tips his head to the side and a smile splits his face from ear to ear showing every one of his razor-sharp teeth. "Of course, it came with a price. Nothing is free, Pet," he growls.

Iroth waves his hand and a vivid memory once more plays in the open air before us, only this time it is his own. I strain at the smoky bonds with no success, causing them to tighten further, nearly blocking my entire airway.

My mother is on the ground only feet from where I am

restrained. She's injured, bleeding from a gash on her head just above her right eye, pushing herself back away from Iroth as he approaches her with slow, determined steps. He lowers himself to his knees and crawls toward her, a wolf descending upon a defenseless rabbit. My mother's eyes are wide with terror. He grabs her by the ankles and forcefully yanks her toward him.

She whimpers, struggling to break free, but he laughs, a deep, cruel sound, and pins her down. She screams for help, but no one comes.

"Oh, come now, Corinne. I just want to play a little game. It's going to be ever so much fun."

I try to turn my face away, not wanting to see what comes next, but Iroth grabs my chin and forces it back to the images with glee.

"You said you wanted to know, Pet. Enjoy the show. I know I will."

He lifts his body over hers until he can place his knees on her arms, restraining her. Iroth brings his face to her eye level, then strokes her cheek with the back of his hand.

"I think we will start with these," he toys, bringing his pointed nail to her left eye. "Eyes are my favorite thing to play with," he remarks.

My mother tries to turn her face away, but he grabs her by the hair with his other hand and forces her head down against the floor, digging his nail into the corner of her eye slowly. Blood gushes from the site as he hooks his finger behind the eye and rips it from its socket, dangling it in front of my mother like a toy on a string. She shrieks with a mixture of terror and pain, kicking and pulling, trying to break her arms free and escape.

"See how they pop?" he asks cheerfully, squeezing the eye in his hand until it squelches. Vitreous humor oozes from between his fingers, and he raises these to his lips, licking the gel-like substance away.

"Please," my mother begs. "Let me go. My baby..."

"Yes, you would like that, wouldn't you?" he mocks. "But you see, magick comes with a price. You asked me to bring your child back from death, and now a life debt must be paid. What is it you witches like to say? As above, so below. Well, my dear, it's time to balance the scales."

"Enough," I squeeze out in a barely audible voice. "I've seen enough."

"Really?" he asks innocently. "But what about this?"

Iroth splays his fingers wide and slams them into my mother's stomach, ripping them down her abdomen and splitting her skin and muscle wide. When he withdraws his fingers, thick blood drips down to the floor beside him, staining the wooden boards.

My mother seizes in pain, howling in agony and he licks his fingers once again, then bends down to her stomach, reaching deep inside and pulling her intestines out, tugging on them like a sailor on rigging. He hums as they slide free, arranging them grotesquely around her body.

The image reminds me so much of what happened to Selena. To see two people I love tortured in such a way threatens to break my resolve.

My mother's eyes roll back into her head in shock, but he slaps her cheek, refusing to let her seek solace in death.

"Not yet, Corinne. We're only getting started. There are so many more organs left to excavate. See? There are the kidneys... and the liver... and my favorite, the heart. I need you alive so you can witness it all. That's so much more fun for me."

Tears stream down my mother's face as she succumbs to his will, unable to fight any longer. Her head rolls to the side, defeated. Iroth plunges his hand into her gaping wound again and again, each time pulling out something new. He leaves the organs attached so that she doesn't bleed out before he is finished, laying them beside her on the floor.

She screams and moans as he empties her body, covering them both in bile and blood. At last, he grabs ahold of her heart while it still beats inside her, slowly squeezing it tighter and tighter with his hand. My mother's face is filled with anguish, but Iroth's shows nothing but pleasure.

"I think I'll take this for myself," he muses, looking down at his hand sunk into the depths of her body. "It will be absolutely delectable. Thank you for playing, Corinne. I had an exquisite time. Game over."

My mother gasps as he rips her heart free, bringing it to his mouth and gnawing on it, like a dog with a raw cut of steak. Her eyes go slack, and she stops fighting as he devours her heart right here on the schoolhouse floor.

"You Hendricks witches are just so much fun!" he cheers, clapping his taloned hands together. "I can't wait to play with you too, Alex. I'm almost thrilled you decided to challenge me. I've been aching for such a delicacy as you."

"I... am not... the one who's... dying here today," I eke out. "You are."

Iroth freezes, eyes widening with incredulity. He stares at me, mouth agape, scanning my face for any hint of fear, but finds none, only fury and determination.

I surge forward, nearly breaking one of my crimson bonds, before being shoved back once more.

Iroth loses control of himself, giving in to his astonished amusement. His deep-bellied laughter rings through the schoolhouse and floods out into the crossroads, filling the silence of the night. He wipes away tears from the corners of his ruby-red eyes.

"Do you really," he starts, fighting back his mirth, "think that you can kill me, Pet?"

I clench my hands into fists and say nothing, drawing my focus inside.

"Me?" he asks, straightening himself up to his full height. "I've walked this Earth for millennia, little witch. I've seen empires fall and brought kings and queens to their knees. I've claimed the souls of hundreds of thousands of you pesky little mortals without breaking a sweat."

He lunges toward me, releasing the bonds so that I am forced to fall forward, grabbing me roughly by the arms and pulling me close.

"I will crush you under my foot like the meaningless insect that you are. I will rip out your bowels and devour your organs. Oh, Alexandria, my little pet. How you amuse me so."

In a flash of movement too quick for me to see, Iroth releases me, lifting his arm and backhanding me across the face. His black talons leave four stinging trails from my eye to my lips. I try to retreat, but he snatches my wrist and flings me toward the doors. I fall to the ground, hard, and groan, forcing myself to maintain my focus as he draws near once again.

"I watched your mother bleed to death on this very spot," he taunts, circling me like a vulture. He draws back his booted foot and slams it into my spine, sending me skittering through the doorway and landing hard on my back on the hard-packed earth.

I watch as he lowers himself onto all fours and crawls toward me as he did with my mother, but this time with a terrifying, disjointed sort of movement. His joints pop and click.

With my feet and elbows, I push myself away from him, trying to create distance between us, but it isn't enough. He catches me by the ankles and halts my escape, tugging my body beneath his own.

"And your grandmother, what an absolute pleasure it was to hear her anguish when she discovered your poor mother's body. It's a rare joy to hear such a symphony of pain. I gorged myself on every last tear, every little whimper. Oh, to see her bent over my masterpiece was a sight to behold."

He straddles my chest and pins my arms beneath his boney knees, digging into my muscles and rendering them useless. I'm no match for his physical strength. Crushed beneath his weight, I can't even wiggle my fingers or clench my fists. But, I've managed to lure him close, which is exactly what I need.

I begin to chant, quietly at first, then louder as Iroth brings his face so close to mine that I can feel his long, thick lashes dart across my forehead. He sticks out his vile, snakelike tongue and licks away a trickle of blood that has escaped from between my lips, moaning as though relishing the flavor.

"Alas, I never had the opportunity to taste Elizabeth. She trapped me in a clever little cage and stole my ring before I had the chance to rip her apart. She was feisty, your grandmother. I imagine her blood is so very full of pepper and spice. Your mother's blood was sweeter, sugar and lilac. But yours, it's dark and rich. Chocolate and honeyed cream."

I turn my head away, but just as he did to my mother, he pulls it back. He lowers his forehead to mine and breathes deeply.

"Fear has a smell, you know. It's a musky sort of scent, heady and oh, so intoxicating." Iroth drags his nose from my ear down to my neck and back. His hot breath assaults me as he whispers, " You reek of terror, Pet. You're positively drowning in it."

It takes everything I have to resist my body's urge to buck and kick, to throw him off balance, to free my numb arms and scramble to my feet. Yet, I force myself to carry on with the chant, keeping his physical form close to the ring.

Tears leak from my eyes as I pray to the Mother, to Hades, to my ancestors, hell, to anyone who is listening, that I somehow make it out of this alive.

He taunts me once more, but I maintain my focus on Iroth's silver ring and ignore his malicious mocking as he hovers over me. I wince as the metal fused to the skin of my thumb reacts to my spell, resisting with such force that it vibrates and heats to a nearly intolerable temperature. Self-preservation warns me to stop now before my magick cannot be undone, but I refuse to give in.

It's now or never. I will not back down.

Iroth pulls away slightly and looks down at me. His eyes bore into mine as he says with a smile, "Your little spell won't save you now. You signed a contract in blood, dear Alex. It's time to pay the price."

With a final word, the vibration stops, settling into a split second of calm before a blast of pure energy radiates through my body and rockets Iroth off of me, sending him flying back. I squeeze my eyes closed as it fills my every cell with an intensity that makes my soul feel like it has been set ablaze.

The containment spell upon the ring is broken. The essences are mine to claim.

CHAPTER TEN

"Now, that was very, very foolish," Iroth growls, standing and recovering from the blast. He swats the dust on his jacket away angrily. "Do you have any idea what you have done? I love this suit."

I pick myself up off the ground, feeling the immense force of the essences rampaging through me. My body is alive with a magick more powerful than anything I have ever wielded. It threads through my muscles and wraps around my bones, setting my nerve endings on fire. I flex my fingers in awe of their new power and lift my eyes to meet his.

He approaches me slowly, cocking his head from side to side in a perfect mimic of his precious hound, examining me closely. Only a few feet away, Iroth stops. His lips curl back into a deriding smile, and with a click of his tongue, he says, "My, Alexandria. What beautiful eyes you have. Would you like to see?"

Iroth snaps his fingers and my reflection appears before me, a misty replica of my own face staring back. My lip is split, and I can see the scratches from his sharp nails running across my cheek, but what startles me the most is my eyes. Once a deep hazel, they are now completely black like oil slicks, all traces of iris and whites vanished.

Iroth laughs, then waves the image away, scattering the mist to the wind.

"It appears you and I are not so different after all," he says with scorn. "But, how did you do it? How did you claim my essence, Pet? I've never seen that done before."

"Wouldn't you like to know?" I answer. My voice is different, too. It's deeper, grating. It thrums with the demonic power of Iroth's essence, tempered only by my grandmother's soothing energy.

I clench my hands into fists, envisioning the red smoke tendrils that held me captive before, letting Iroth's energy flow into my fingers and calling them forth. The smoke rises around me, roiling and stretching into thick tendrils, now at my command. "This ends tonight."

"Indeed, I believe it will." Iroth circles me, spinning and dancing gayly as if seeing his demonic essence harvested and used against him brings him nothing but joy. "But, you didn't listen to me, Pet. What a shame. What a shame."

"I will never listen to you. You're a monster!" I yell, sending a tendril of magick in his direction with as much force as I can muster, but he easily jumps aside.

"A monster? Well, that's really a question of perception, isn't it? Look at you now, Alex. You wield my power against me. What does that make you?"

I don't answer. Instead, I withdraw the athame from my pocket and race toward him, moving at speeds faster than I ever thought humanly capable. When I reach him, I slash out violently, letting rage power my movements. Iroth spins away, but the blade knicks his face, drawing a thin line of blood from beneath the skin. He summons his own magick to shove me back with ease, then touches his fingertip to the small wound.

"Ouch," he says with disinterest. "Whatever will I do with a wound such as this? Honestly, Pet. You're going to have to do so much better than that."

"I... will... destroy... you!" I yell, breaking free from his magick's hold as I race forward again, this time sending two tendrils after his arms. They wrap around his wrists and haul him up off the ground, leaving him dangling before me. He doesn't even try to fight.

"Will you?" he asks, nonchalantly. "Perhaps. But, I'd wager my soul... if I still had one... that it is not me you are destroy-ing." His voice is calm, too calm for my liking as he continues. "Tell me, what do you know of the magick that bound my essence to the ring?"

"I know enough," I answer, stalking toward him in the same predatory manner he so often uses with me.

"Mmm, that's a very vague answer," he replies, lips thin-ning into a fine line. "Let's start with one simple question: do you know what your grandmother has done?"

Hatred settles into my chest as I reach him, a hatred so potent that it feels tangible inside me. "She bound your life to her own."

"Indeed!" he says with a wicked grin. "Indeed, she did. So, now that you're siphoning my essence, what do you imagine you are doing to her, Pet?"

I will the tendrils to tighten, watching as they twist and contract. The bones in his wrist grind together, and for the first time, Iroth seems a bit uncomfortable. He clenches his hands into fists, then flexes his fingers, grimacing.

Between gritted teeth, he calls, "How is dear, sweet grand-mother doing? I know you can feel her inside of you. Is she strong? Fighting fit? The irony is so very exquisite."

I roar and barrel forward, plunging the athame into his chest, burying the blade hilt deep. Slick, hot blood spurts as I remove the blade, plunging it into him again and again. I expect Iroth to squirm or try to fight, but he doesn't. He doesn't even make a sound. I look up at him, only to find him grinning lazily.

"I tire of this game," he announces. Horrified, I watch as he twists his wrists and the tendrils snap, dissolving into thin air. "As I said before, you don't understand the rules of the game you are playing."

I blink and he vanishes, nowhere to be seen, just as he had all those years ago. Fear floods through my system, and I back away, searching the darkness for his form.

"Sure, you've picked up some neat party tricks, Pet," he calls out from several feet away, appearing out of thin air. "But, do you know how to do THIS?" Iroth shouts, flinging his arm and hurling a powerful, invisible force into me.

I tumble backward, rolling through the dirt until my back slams into the trunk of an old Maple behind me.

"Oh, I can do much better than that. How about THIS!"

He raises his arms above his head and my body lifts up off of the ground, hovering in the air as though it is weightless. With a violent gesture, he lowers his arms, slamming me down with such force that my skull bounces off the earth with a sickening crack.

The world around me spins, and I struggle to push myself into a seated position. Blood trickles down my face from a gash across my nose. I groan.

Iroth crosses the space between us and kneels before me, trailing his fingers in little circles through the dirt. "What's the matter, Pet? Feeling a little sick, maybe? Tired? Should we just settle your debt now? I'm working up quite an appetite."

"Hardly," I challenge, forcing myself to my feet.

Iroth mirrors my movements, rising steadily alongside me.

I reach for the essence swirling at my core and pull it to the surface. Power surges through my palms as I summon the same invisible force, shoving it into him and knocking him back, then pounce, pushing him against an old Oak and pinning him there with my own magick, strengthened by the cool resolve of my grandmother's essence. I bring the athame to his throat, digging the point of the blade into the soft space under his chin and pushing hard. I'm met with resistance as he pushes it away with his power, and the blade refuses to penetrate his skin.

"You forget, little witch. I have had millennia to hone my abilities. What have you had? All of fifteen minutes? You're weak, and your power is fading. You won't be able to fend me off for long."

"I don't need to," I grunt. "I just need long enough."

Iroth's brow furrows in confusion, and now it's my turn to smile. I may not have the grasp on his abilities that he does, but I do have everything, every drop of the essences, from the ring.

I call upon my grandmother's essence, feeling it churn inside my chest. There isn't much left now. By siphoning it off to fuel my magickal boost, I'm burning it up. But, her mortal life is tied to her essence, and with each drop drained, I'm pushing her closer to her demise. She's letting go, passing on, and when she dies, Iroth will become mortal, too.

The moment he realizes the sacrifice I am making, that I have chosen to drain what remains of my grandmother's life force to weaken him, he roars, fury breaking in waves over the crossroads.

I am forced to drop him to the ground, but I brace myself this time, prepared for the wave of energy that emanates from his scream. Losing my grip on the athame, I cross my arms and dig my heels into the dirt, shielding myself. I strain as I slip back an inch at a time, breathing through the pressure.

Behind me, trees sway and crack, tumbling over each other into the forest.

"You worthless little worm!" he bellows, grabbing me by the shoulders and sending me flying back toward the school. "I will crush you! I can't wait to see the light drain from your eyes. I will devour..."

He trails off as I feel it, the final pulse of my grandmother's essence, then a gaping emptiness where her energy had been. Iroth's eyes widen with fear, and he slashes out with his taloned fingers, but before they make contact, they change, shrinking down into the pointed black nails he wore before.

He staggers backward, staring at his hands and clutching his chest as blood seeps from the wounds I inflicted earlier.

"CeCe!" he calls out to the hound. "CeCe! Annihilate this stupid witch! Come out and play!"

But the hound doesn't come. It sits there at the entrance to the building, staring between the two of us, head flicking back and forth in confusion. It sniffs the air and narrows its eyes. A low, deep growl emanates from the beast's mouth, but it isn't growling at me.

"I command you!" Iroth bellows. "Devour this woman. Claim her soul."

A rumbling chuckle echoes through the crossroads as the hound raises its head high. It snaps its maw and licks its lips pointedly in Iroth's direction, then turns away, leaving the crossroads behind.

"You're not a demon anymore," I answer as Iroth drops to his knees. "You're just an insect like the rest of us humans. How does it feel, Iroth? You'll die right here, in the middle of the crossroads where you've ruined the lives of so many. You're right. The irony is so *very* exquisite."

Iroth collapses into a heap on the ground, straining for air through his punctured lungs. I fall to my knees beside him, watching him struggle.

After a moment, he manages to speak.

"How... does it feel?" Iroth asks with a gasp as I lean over him. He chokes on his own blood, then smiles widely at me with crimson-stained teeth. "Is all well with your soul?"

"Heavenly," I answer sarcastically, but it only makes him laugh and sputter more.

"I don't think so," he wheezes.

"Really, because it feels like a miracle come true to see you pay for everything you've done."

I narrow my eyes, feeling his life force slip away.

"I sincerely doubt, Pet," he breathes, "that you'll ever know what any form of Heaven feels like."

Iroth's eyes roll back and he convulses, teeth grinding and mouth foaming. Then, as though his body is a machine that has run out of gas, his seizing slows gradually to a stop. Iroth's head lolls to the side and his body stills. I lean back on my heels and stare in disbelief.

He's dead, really and truly dead.

I watch as his body crumbles to ash, retaining form at first, but as a light breeze blows through the trees, it disintegrates and scatters on the wind.

It has cost me everything, but it's over. My mother's death and Selena's torment have been avenged. My grandmother's energy can finally rest. Potent sadness and disbelief ravage me, forcing wet sobs from my chest.

The demon Iroth is no more. I won.

CHAPTER ELEVEN

MY GRANDMOTHER'S AIDES FIND HER IN HER BED THE NEXT MORNING, and as far as they are concerned, she passed peacefully in her sleep. Only I know the truth: I am responsible for her death, and that is something I will be forced to live with for the rest of my days.

The other practitioners in our Coven have helped me prepare her final rites. We constructed the pyre of Yew and Willow, wrapping a carefully braided rope of flowers around the rectangular base: Violets, Gardenias, Roses, and Hibiscus. Before placing my grandmother's body on the platform, I sprinkle a touch of my mother's ashes across the top so that they may be together for all of their days in the hereafter. Our priestess blesses the wood, consecrating it for the final rite, and a woman whom I have never met, dressed in our formal ceremonial garb, helps me place my only remaining family member upon the pyre, squeezing my shoulder gently as we back away.

We take our turns sharing memories of my grandmother, and so many wonderful things are said. The priestess splashes an anointing oil across her shroud, her favorite throw that I almost ruined when Iroth first came to claim me. The oil smells of lavender and chamomile, meant to soothe the grief of those left behind. I hold back tears, not only of sadness but of guilt, as I lay the torch to the pyre and say my final goodbyes.

I watch her body burn until late into the night. It crumbles into nothing but bits of shattered bone amongst the charred branches, uncomfortably reminding me of Iroth's ashes.

As the deepest, darkest part of night falls, I wend my way back through the woods to my home, climbing up onto the side porch and sitting in our rickety wooden porch swing, watching the stars blink in and out.

For a time, I allow myself to grieve. I never wanted to hurt my grandmother, but I tell myself that she was ready to pay the ultimate price. She said as much in the letter she left behind for me to find. She had spent so many years fading away to nothing but a shadow of herself. It must have been agony. I convince myself that I'm almost glad her suffering has ended. Denial is a powerful thing.

Behind me, a twig snaps from the depths of the darkened forest, drawing me back to the moment. I sit up straight, squinting at the edge of the woods, trying to find the source of the sound, but the noise never comes again. Soothed by the absence of further disruption, I lean back in the swing and close my eyes.

"What a beautiful night," a voice sounds next to me.

I shoot up and jump out of the swing, turning to see a familiar young woman sitting right next to where I had been just seconds before.

"Selena?" I ask, thoroughly shocked and confused.

"Selena?" she answers, brow furrowed in bemusement.

"Yes," I prompt. "When did you get here? How did you get here?"

"Right," Selena replies. "That's what I called myself before."

"Before?"

"Yes, before. Back when I sent Iroth here to do my bidding." She chuckles softly, as if in remembrance. "Forgive my memory. I've been busy since we last spoke."

My mouth falls open in horror as I take a tentative step back, but Selena pats the seat beside her, and my legs move forward of their own volition. I stare at the woman who was once my friend, someone whom I haven't spoken to in years, and she looks at me with a polite smile, much like a doctor would at a dying patient's bedside.

"I've shown you a courtesy by giving you time to grieve your loss," she says, reaching out to take my hand in her own. Iroth's ring is still fused to my thumb, and she strokes it, almost lovingly, as she continues, "but, the time for leniency is through. You have not held up your end of the deal, Alexandria. The favor was given, but the price was not paid."

"Deal? Price?" I ask, unable to form a coherent sentence.

"The terms of the contract you struck with my poor, deceased Iroth were very clear. You owed him a favor, completed to his satisfaction, or you owed him a soul to do with as he pleased. As Iroth is no more, it stands to reason that you did not uphold your part of the agreement."

"How do you know about this?" I ask, suddenly incredibly uncomfortable. I try to pull my hand away, but Selena grips it tightly in her own, so tightly that my fingers begin to throb.

"How do I know? Why, because I wrote the contract, silly thing!" she answers gleefully. "Did you truly think that Iroth was the only demon to whom you are beholden? Iroth may have held the contract while he was still alive, but his essence belonged to me. Therefore, any deal you struck with my demon, is a deal struck with myself, and I am not one to allow a binding agreement to be cast aside."

"No, that doesn't make sense. You were a little girl, like me."

"And Iroth was a little boy," she says, looking at me empathetically. "What difference does that make, Alex? A body is only a physical embodiment of the essence. You know that."

"But, you were my friend. We grew up together. You lived just down the road from me for years! We played in the woods and pretended to be teachers in the schoolhouse. You're not saying that…"

She cuts me off, growing bored with my unwillingness to accept the truth. "Yes, yes. That's all true enough, I suppose. The form I borrowed did age alongside you, and we did play together for a time. It was a very long game for me. I'm glad it's finally coming to an end."

"No," I choke out, eyes wide with horror.

"Yes," she answers with a smirk.

"But, Iroth is gone. The contract is void," I stammer, pleading with my eyes. "It's over."

"True, in some ways you have won. You have forced my hand, so here I am, appearing before you in person, forced to once again inhabit this pitiful excuse for a mortal so that I may claim my payment. But, the payment remains mine to claim. After all these years and all of that careful training Elizabeth gave you, you still failed to heed your grandmother's warning, Alexandria. Magick always comes with a price."

"I paid the price. I paid it with my grandmother's life!" I shout, trying to rise from the swing, but she reaches out her other hand and pins my legs down with ease.

"Her life was not yours to claim," she answers calmly. "And Iroth's essence was not yours to destroy. There are rules, Alexandria. I will not allow them to be broken."

In a swift movement, she picks up the hand with the ring and holds it between both of her own, squeezing so tightly that I'm certain my bones will break within her grip. She smiles at me, then tilts her head down menacingly. Ruby red flashes behind her eyes. I gulp, unwilling to believe this is happening.

"I don't want to die," I whisper, cowardice lacing my voice.

"Oh, you're not going to die," she answers. A malicious grin spreads across her face, distorting Selena's features into a gruesome mask. "In fact, you're going to live for a very long time."

The silver band on my thumb vibrates and heats, just as it did when my spell freed the essences from their containment. A sick, swirling nausea bubbles within me, and the air in my lungs is sucked away. I struggle to breathe, feeling my heart rate climb immeasurably. Fiery pain begins in my hand and spreads through my body, scorching my nerves and sending wave after wave of absolute agony through me. I choke and try to pull away.

"Iroth's deal never specified what kind of torture you would be forced to endure should you fail to meet his demands, and I've thought of just the thing," she says calmly, boring her eyes into my own. "What better way could there be to torture you, a devoted witch who wanted nothing more than to avenge the deaths of her mother, and now her grandmother, than to turn you into the creature you hated most."

"No!" I gasp, feeling the essence of my magick draining steadily from my body. Its absence leaves a void, a hollowness the likes of which I have never felt.

"Oh, yes," she croons. "Yes, it's just the thing. You will take Iroth's place at the crossroads for eternity. One essence for another."

Before I can speak, the stars in the sky wink out, replaced

by utter blackness. I am drowning in fear, helpless in her grasp, like a fly caught in a spider's web.

"Rest now, Alexandria," I hear as I fall into a deep slumber, her words echoing in my ears. "We have many millennia together, you and I. You'll need your strength to claim my souls. As above, so below, like you witches always say." The burning in the ring suddenly stops, replaced by an icy cold. "The circle is sealed."

Her manic laughter is the last thing I hear as my consciousness fades away, and I remember myself no more.

THANK YOU FOR READING

Thank you for reading *Dealings in the Dark*. I hope you have enjoyed this work.

Do you have questions for the author? If so, reach out to me at smoran@obsidianinkwell.com and you might have them answered!

Please feel free to leave an honest review on Amazon or Goodreads. I look forward to writing for you again soon!

Find *Dealings in the Dark* on Amazon

Find *Dealings in the Dark* on Goodreads

QUESTIONS FOR THE AUTHOR

Q) WHAT MADE YOU WANT TO WRITE A STORY ABOUT A DEAL WITH a demon?

Even as a young child, I have always been fascinated by the supernatural. My fascination comes from both sides of my family, as my mother has been a huge fan of horror stories for as long as I can remember and my father has an interest in supernatural creatures and magick. Plus, I love to write about supernatural things during Spooky Season each year.

The idea of being careful when interacting with magick, or anything else in the supernatural "realm," is important because I am a firm believer that if you don't know what you're doing, you could do something very dangerous. Outside of magick, this same concept still applies. I wouldn't want someone who doesn't know how to operate performing open-heart surgery on someone I love! So, long story short, I just love supernatural things and never miss a chance to emphasize a good lesson. After all, my degree is in education!

. . .

Q) How do you pronounce the name Iroth?

I went back and forth many times when I was deciding on the pronunciation of Iroth's name. When I think of my character, I imagine the pronunciation as "eye-roth," but the beauty of reading is that the pronunciation ultimately belongs to you, the reader! I have heard "Ee-roth" and "Eye-rowth," too!

Q) Does Alexandria follow the Christian religion and believe in Heaven and Hell?

It's true that Alex is a practitioner of magick, and through her interactions with the deities upon her grandmother's altar, it is clear that she and her family are polytheistic.

With that said, there is no statement made in this text that denounces the Christian God or that indicates Alex does not believe in the concept of either Heaven or Hell. Very likely, as many modern practitioners do, Alex and her family see the Christian God as another possible deity for worship, and that Heaven and Hell are afterlives associated with worship of this specific deity.

In my drafting process, I chose to represent two deities, Hecate and Hades, who are associated with crossings, since the bulk of the story focuses on deals made with a crossroads demon.

Furthermore, there is an emphasis in this novella on the presence of a female deity, often referred to as the Mother. This deity could be interpreted as any female deity across any pantheon or culture, and that is intentional. In my mind, this most closely refers to Hecate, as she is presented on the altar. I focused specifically on female worship since magick is most commonly associated with female practitioners, and all of Alex's essential family members are female. It is, however, important to note that magickal practice can be done by anyone of any gender. My focus on female practitioners is not intended to exclude any other practitioners.

Q) WHY IS **Alex so afraid of the hellhound if she's a witch?**

In mythology, the hellhound is traditionally seen as an omen of death. Though hell hounds have been alternately viewed as helpful and harmful, those who see them are typically fated to a death that they cannot escape.

As a practitioner of magick, Alex would be aware of this and fearful that no matter what she did, she couldn't escape an early demise.

Also, hellhounds are terrifying. I would not want to be Alex in Chapter Three or Chapter Nine. Would you? The very thought gives me the shivers!

Q) WHY DID **you choose to represent magick in the manner that you did?**

I wanted to represent magick in a way that was closer to the traditional truth of witchcraft practices wherein the user sets intentions, relies on magickal tools such as herbs and stones, and performs spells and rituals that don't necessarily have an immediate, tangible effect. However, I also needed to incorporate a form of magick usage that made Alex's family practice more interesting and propel the story forward. So, I chose to incorporate elements of traditional magick and the kind of magick often presented in modern tales of fiction to achieve this balance.

Q) IS THERE **a reason you chose to write this story as a novella instead of a full length novel?**

I actually started this novella with the idea that it would be a short story, much like my first publication, "Stages of Grief." However, as the writing progressed, it became clear to me that there was more that needed to be said about Alex and her journey.

I wanted to publish this story at a specific time of year and wasn't really ready to commit to another full length novel since I was still editing my first novel's manuscript when I began drafting. Thus, the idea of presenting Alex's conundrum in the format of a novella was born.

Q) Will you be continuing Alex's story now that this one is over?

When I originally published this novella, my answer was that I simply did not know if I would ever continue with the series. However, after receiving feedback from readers and requests for both prequels and sequels, my answer quickly changed to yes! At this time, there are four planned novellas in this series. There may be even more by the time I am finished.

Bound and Betrayed, book two of the Cursed Souls series, releases in January of 2023.

Q) What will you be working on next?

My plan is to move forward with editing the draft of my manuscript for my full length novel, *The Ruin*. After that, I don't know! I have at least two more novellas in the Cursed Souls series to write, and I'd love to get more short stories out into the world, too. If you would like to keep up with my work, please visit www.samanthamoran.net and subscribe to my mailing list. You'll receive monthly emails from me regarding progress, deals, and more.

Do you have questions for the author?

If you have questions for me about this text, please reach out to me at smoran@obsidianinkwell.com or visit my website at www.samanthamoran.net and you just might have them answered!

THANK you for reading *Dealings in the Dark*! I hope you enjoyed this novella. Please feel free to leave an honest review on Amazon and/or Goodreads. I look forward to writing for you again soon!

Acknowledgments

I would like to thank my friends, Marissa and Mike, for encouraging me to pursue my dreams as a writer at a time when I rarely spent my energy on caring for myself.

I would like to thank my husband, John, for being a constant listener and second pair of eyes. By now, I'm sure you've already heard every part of this story six or seven times, and I haven't even published it yet. Also, thank you for supporting my dreams and encouraging me to buy Vellum.

I'd also like to thank authors Charlie Nottingham and Tatum Holt for listening to me and giving me advice at the start of my writing career. We have never met in person, but I hope to meet you both someday.

Finally, I'd like to thank photographer Ashley Klaasen for taking such a great photograph that I can use in my many works to come. Each of you has made this work possible.

BONUS CONTENT: BOUND AND BETRAYED

Thank you for reading *Dealings in the Dark*, the first installment in the Cursed Souls series. Enjoy this excerpt from *Bound and Betrayed*, the next book in the series.

Bound and Betrayed
Samantha Moran
Book Two of the
Cursed Souls series

CHAPTER ONE

MONDAY AFTERNOON

"Selena?"

Dr. Holland's voice draws me back to reality. Without even knowing, I had been lost in thought.

How long have I been dissociating?

"Hmm? Sorry…"

"You were far away for a little while. Where did you go?"

"I…" I begin, but the words die on my tongue.

Dr. Holland waits patiently as I stare at the tip of my shoe and draw circles on her otherwise perfect shag rug. I know she's watching me. She's always watching and waiting during our sessions.

"I'm sorry," I continue. "I'm tired."

"Have you been sleeping well? Still having nightmares?"

I nod. I've been having nightmares for eighteen years. It seems unlikely to change anytime soon.

"Do you want to talk about them?" Her voice is calm and gentle, as always.

For the last five years, Dr. Holland has been my psychiatrist. She's the most recent in a long line of counselors, therapists, psychologists, and psychiatrists, each possessing or preferring a different title. She's the best one I've had so far.

It took them eight years to let me out of my in-patient treatment. When I became an adult and demonstrated no plans or desire to harm myself or others, the treatment center had no legal reason to hold me any longer.

There were so many different doctors and nurses in the facility that I've lost count. None of them listened, though. None of them helped.

When I was released, my parents found Dr. Llovero. I didn't like him at all. He was pushy, always asking the wrong questions. He treated me like a child. I stopped seeing him after nearly a year. My parents were profoundly disappointed.

The next one was Dr. Branson. She was okay. I found her online. I didn't have to leave my room for our appointments. I liked that. It felt safer. She and I made progress for a time, but then she got married and had to leave the practice because she moved out of state. That was difficult. I don't like being left behind.

Dr. Holland came after her. I like Dr. Holland well enough. She listens to me, like actually listens. She doesn't interrupt and ask stupid questions. She waits and watches. Sometimes she watches for a very long time without saying a word. It was uncomfortable at first, but I've gotten used to it now. I have to come to her office for our visits, but she has a nice, welcoming space.

The couches here are soft, not like the leather ones that Dr. Llovero had in his office. They don't creak when I move or stick to my legs when I wear shorts. There are plenty of blankets and pillows around in case I get cold or want to hide behind them.

One of the pillows is a very bright blue and shaped like a heart. That's my favorite.

I like the art on the walls, too. There are lots of drawings from her younger patients and some cool paintings and photographs from her older ones. She even hung one of mine.

Last year, I took a picture of an old treehouse in the woods. I don't know how I found it. It felt like I had been there a thousand times before. My feet simply carried me back and back, past the running creek and a freaky old abandoned building.

The treehouse looked like the usual kind of place where kids used to play. The walls were painted sloppily. There were crayon drawings near the bottom. There was even a raggedy old curtain that served as a door. It waved to me in the wind. I think that's why I climbed up. It was almost like being invited. I know that seems silly, but it's true.

The idea of the treehouse was striking, I guess. I could picture a small group of kids up there playing during the long, hot, summer days. But, it hadn't been taken care of in a while. Something about the way it looked, the emptiness of it, resonated with me. So, I crouched in the doorway under the shredded fabric and snapped the picture.

I printed one copy and hung it up on my wall. I stared at that picture for a month before I brought Dr. Holland a copy, too. She politely thanked me and set it up in a nice bronze frame, then hung it up by the window directly across from the couch.

I keep waiting for her to ask me about the picture, but she hasn't yet. I stare at it for a while and wonder why that stupid picture matters so much. I don't know yet. I'll figure it out eventually.

Dr. Holland says that we figure most things out eventually. Maybe she'll figure me out. I hope so.

"Selena?" she prompts me again.

"Yeah, sorry. I'm... Sorry. I guess I don't really remember much about what happened in the dream last night. I just remember how it made me feel."

"That happens to me after nightmares, too. Feelings tend to linger longer than the events themselves. Can you tell me about how you felt?"

I reach for the heart-shaped pillow and hold it on my lap, leaning back against the couch. The little pillow has a patch of sequins that change colors when you flip them. I drag my fingers through them, watching the colors change.

"I was afraid."

"Okay. Do you remember why?"

I squeeze my eyes shut and concentrate, trying to drift back into the memory of the dream. "I remember... running. I was running from something."

"What were you running from?"

I try to picture it, but whatever it was won't come into focus. "I don't remember. I'm sorry."

"Don't push yourself too hard. Let your mind still. If you're meant to remember, it will come to you."

'*Let my mind still.*' She uses that phrase a lot. I try. I do. But, it doesn't always work. Maybe I'm doing something wrong? That doesn't surprise me at all. I never seem to do the right thing.

"Practice your breath work," she reminds me. "Breathe in, hold, and release."

I do. It helps a little.

"I don't think it was a person."

"Good. What do you think it was?"

"I don't know. An animal? A dog, maybe?"

"You dream of dogs often. Would it surprise you if you were having a nightmare about a dog?"

"No."

I do dream of dogs a lot. Not the soft, lovable kind. I like those well enough. My parents used to have one when I was growing up. They even brought him to visit me at the facility a couple of times. His name was Max. I thought it was kind of a stupid name. We played in the courtyard and I scratched him behind the ears. He was funny. He kicked the ground so hard when he got scratches. I liked him.

No, my nightmares aren't filled with dogs like Max. They're filled with the kind of dogs that have horrifying rows of razor-sharp teeth, lines and lines of them like sharks.

Dr. Holland says that the freaky dogs from my dreams aren't real. She says they're just a manifestation of childhood fears. I want to believe her. Max didn't have teeth like that, and I don't think I've ever met a dog that did. But, I don't know. I have no idea why I dream of terrifying dogs. There's so much that I can't remember. I wish I could tell what's real and what's not. My life would be so much easier if I could trust my own mind.

I've never known what that feels like. So many people have told me that the things I see and hear, the things that feel so real, are figments of my imagination. They have to be right. It's me against all of them. They have the numbers. I'm all alone.

I reign myself in. A pity party won't solve anything. I've wasted too much time lost in my thoughts during this session already.

"I remember that it was late at night. And, it was so cold. The kind of cold that lets you see your breath. I was breathing so hard. The little clouds kept getting in the way. I had to keep swatting at them, but the more I swatted, the thicker they got."

"In your dream or when you were awake?" she asks.

"In my dream."

She scribbles something on her paper, then looks up and gives me a reassuring smile.

"And there was this strange laughter. Someone was laughing at me."

"Laughing?" she asks, shifting in her chair and taking notes.

"Yeah, laughing. It wasn't scary by itself, the laughing. But, with the dog... Well, I think it was a dog. I don't know. It sounded cruel, I guess? Like, the woman was happy that I was so scared..."

"Did you recognize the woman's voice? Was it someone you knew?"

"Sort of," I answer. "It was very familiar, but I can't quite place the voice. I don't know if it belongs to a real person or not."

"Mmm." She scribbles something else down, then sits the pad of paper on her lap.

"I don't think I remember anything else."

"That's fine. You've done well today, Selena. I know it's hard to talk about your dreams. Thank you for sharing this with me."

I nod. She's right. It is hard to talk about stuff like this. People already think I'm crazy. I see things that they don't see, and I hear things that others don't. Well, I used to anyway. Now I take about six different medications to keep the hallucinations at bay. But, people around town know. If I say the wrong thing... I trust Dr. Holland well enough, but word gets around. I've learned that the walls can have ears. I'm tired of the stares and the whispers. More importantly, I don't want to get sent back to the treatment center.

The treatment center was awful. I'll take the nightmares and whispers from the shadows over a stay at the facility any day.

Dr. Holland glances down at her watch. "We've run out of time today. Do you feel like you need another session tomorrow to talk about this dream, or should we keep with our regular Thursday appointment?"

"Thursday will be fine."

"I'm going to think about this dream. I want to look over some of our past sessions to see if I can help you draw any connections to things we've discussed before. Would it be alright if we spoke more about it on Thursday, then?"

"Sure," I answer. I set the pillow aside and begin to stand.

"Selena?" Dr. Holland interjects.

I stop and look up. Her usual kind smile is plastered on her face. I used to think it was fake. I'm not sure anymore. She seems nice. Things aren't always what they seem, though.

"Have you been drinking your water and taking your medications like we talked about?"

I blush. I knew she wouldn't let me get away without it.

"I try. I don't like the way some of the pills make me feel."

"I understand," she says. She clicks her shiny black pen, sending the tip back inside. "I want you to try though, especially with your new medication. It will take some time to adjust. If it isn't taken properly, it won't work as it should. Can you try again?"

"I will." I turn to walk toward the office door.

"While we are on the topic of medications, let's try to take some time off from the sleeping pills this week. Just for a few days, okay?"

"Why?" I ask. "I need them." My hand is on the doorknob, but I don't turn it.

"Sometimes, they can make dreams more intense. If the nightmares are bothering you more lately, it might be helpful to take a short break. Just for a few days."

That makes sense, I guess. I could use a break from the vivid dreams. The problem is, I can't sleep without the pills. I take them every night. I have since I was ten. Without them, I doubt I'll even be able to sleep at all.

I don't want to argue about them with Dr. Holland. If I do, she might stop prescribing them altogether. I can't have that. So instead, I just say, "Okay."

"Okay." Dr. Holland stands and moves behind her desk.

She unlocks the drawer and drops the notepad inside, then retrieves another, probably for her next patient. She always takes her notes on paper. I like that. I don't know why.

"Don't forget to do your journal work," she prompts as I step into the hall. "I'll see you on Thursday!"

I pull the office door closed behind me and pass through the small waiting room, making my way to the exit. An older, balding man smiles at me as I pass. I see him here often. He seems nice enough, I guess. We don't talk though. Patients aren't supposed to talk to each other. Not that I would want to, anyway...

Before I make it outside, Dr. Holland greets him warmly.

"Stanley, it's good to see you. Come on in."

I see him stand and collect his things, then disappear into Dr. Holland's office. She flashes one more reassuring smile at me before she closes the door behind her.

I check my phone. The bus will be here in about ten minutes. Out of habit, I dig my earbuds out of my pocket and stick them in. I use these every day, too. The world can be too much sometimes. Too many voices. Too many sudden noises. Too many people watching me.

I open up my music on my phone and it immediately starts playing. The heavy beat drowns out the noise of the passing train. I stuff my hands into my pockets and check for traffic. Breathing in the humid early autumn air, I head off in the direction of the bus stop.

OCTOBER 4TH

Mom and dad are leaving for Colorado in the morning. They'll be gone until Sunday for Andrea's wedding. I'll have to fend for myself for the next few days.

I can do this. I think...

At least I have leftover lasagna. Mom's lasagna has always been my favorite food. She makes everything from scratch. It's gooey and hot, and all-around delicious. She grows her own tomatoes and fresh garlic out back to make huge pots of sauce every summer. She uses the fresh herbs she grows on the kitchen windowsill, too. Her grandmother taught her how to do that when she was little, and she's tried to teach me, but I've never been very good at it. I burnt the sauce once. She stopped asking me to help after that.

Tonight though, I know that she only made it because she feels guilty that she and dad are leaving for their trip in the morning. There are enough leftovers to feed a family of ten, even though it's just the three of us.

It's always been just the three of us. That's my fault. They wanted to have another kid before I ended up in the treatment center. They stopped trying after that. I can't blame them, I suppose. Who would want another kid when their first kid turned out like me?

I'm twenty-eight years old, and they're still afraid to leave me home alone for more than twenty-four hours. I still require supervision. It makes me feel like a burden.

I am a burden.

Mom will never admit that, though. She's the most selfless person I know. That makes it even worse. I wish I could be a normal adult and move out, give her back her own life. But, I need my parents. I can't live alone.

I'll just have to be extra convincing tomorrow so that she doesn't cancel their trip. They deserve a break from constantly monitoring me.

Dr. Holland suggested that I should stop taking my sleeping pills for a little while because of how bad the nightmares have been. She says that the pills can make the dreams worse. I don't know if it's better to take the pills and sleep, even if I still have nightmares, or to not take the pills and stay awake all night. I know that's what's going to happen. I can't sleep without them.

I shouldn't be afraid of the dark. That's what everyone says, anyway. They tell me I don't have to be afraid of the shadows anymore. I want to believe them. I'm trying to believe them. It's just... sometimes the shadows whisper to me.

I will try not to take them tonight. I hope she's right.

Find Bound and Betrayed *on Amazon*

Also by Samantha Moran

Cursed Souls:

Dealings in the Dark, (2022)

Bound and Betrayed, (2022)

Legacy of Lies, Coming Soon

Standalone Works:

Tales of Grief and Healing, (2023)

The Ruin, (2023)

For the Dark and Depraved:

Wicked Little Rabbit, (2024)

The Apothecary of Curiosities Short Stories:

"Death's Nell," (2023)

"Kiss of Death," (2023)

"Deadly Delicacies," (2024)

About the Author

Photo Credit: Ashley Klaasen Photography

Samantha Moran (she/her) is a multi-genre author primarily focused on supernatural horror, thriller, and fantasy. She is fascinated by all manner of things that go bump in the night and strives to create relatable characters who face realistic problems in fictional settings. As her motto claims, she is a firm believer in the idea that "happily ever after is overrated" and prefers her stories to be full of twists and mysteries.

Samantha holds a Bachelor's in English Secondary Education and is a proud Magna Cum Laude graduate of Western Michigan University. (Go Broncos!) She is also a loving mother of two amazing children and has been happily married to her husband since 2015. She and her family reside in southwest

Michigan, though she has also previously resided in the Balti-more, Maryland area.

Samantha lives with Multiple Sclerosis which sometimes severely impacts her daily life, especially her ability to use her hands.

In her free time, she loves tarot, playing *Dungeons and Dragons*, reading books, writing, and spending time with her family and pets.

For more information about Samantha Moran, visit her website at www.samanthamoran.net.

Visit Samantha Moran's website